POWER HUNGRY

WANDA SWAN

Power Hungry: The Queen's Court, Book 1

Copyright © 2022 by Wanda Swan and Black Swan Publishing

Editor: Maggie Morris, Indie Editor

Cover Design: Stephanie Saw, Seventhstar Art

Proofreaders: Aislin Lynx, Megan Breininger

To Brooke, and all the women brave enough to start a new adventure.

TRIGGER WARNING

Themes of child abuse and sexual assault are present in this book. These themes are shown as memories only and are not graphic.

Please be aware if these are triggers for you.

PROLOGUE

THREE MONTHS AGO—A CONVERSATION between the ruler of a foreign court and his son.

"The time is now." The father sits behind the large mahogany desk in his dark, wood-paneled office.

"So soon?" The son pours three fingers of scotch into two cut crystal tumblers at the bar. With drinks in hand, he strolls over to his father and hands him a glass. Then he lowers himself resignedly into the leather chair opposite his father's desk.

The father gently swirls the scotch in the tumbler, enjoying the aroma that's released. "I know what I'm asking might take you away from your work for a little while, but it can't be helped. And it won't be for long."

The son holds his glass up for inspection. "I'll do what needs to be done. I won't let you down."

"I know you won't." The father gifts his son with a look of paternal pride before putting down his drink and rustling through the papers on his desk. Finding the one he wants, he picks it up and meets his son's eyes with a weighted stare. "She's graduating from Brown University this May, and then she'll be leaving Providence. Leaving Earthside and going back to Avalon. You need to make her fall in love with you, submit to you before then. Use any means necessary."

The son sprawls in the chair, letting his arms hang lazily over the sides and stretching his long legs out in front of him. "I already said I'll take care of it."

"She must agree to marry you. We need the power that will come from aligning our family with hers. Without her family's power, we can't move forward with our plans. We must have that power."

"She'll agree to marry me." The son chuckles. "I'll lure her in, make her surrender to me." The son's eyes harden, and his voice lowers as he says, "But I'll be married to her in name only. I have no plans to settle down. I'll put her in a house in our territory and visit her from time to time."

"What you do with her after your marriage is your business. My only interest is her family's power. As long as you don't do anything to jeopardize that and you maintain control of her, you may do as you please."

"She'll be as docile and obedient as a little lamb." The son raises his drink. "Like a lamb to the slaughter. It'll be easy. It's as good as done."

The father picks up his scotch and raises it to his son. "I'll drink to that."

CHAPTER ONE

H E'S STALKING ME.

My lips compress in annoyance as I pull my buzzing phone out of my back pocket. This had better not be another text from Ash. *He's so annoying.*

I first met Ash when we were kids, but we've never been friends, and our paths haven't crossed in more than fifteen years. I wouldn't be able to pick him out of a line up.

Then a couple of months ago, he started texting me. Asking me to go out for coffee or have dinner with him. At first, I made up excuses like "I'm studying for a final" or "I have a paper due". But he didn't take the hint, so I gave him a firm "No thanks" and then stopped responding to him altogether. When he continued to pester me, I changed my number, which had been a major pain in the ass.

Checking my phone, I see the message isn't from Ash. *Thank fuck.* It's a group text from a guy in my international finance study group, confirming he reserved a room in the library for us tonight.

I'm walking around the Wriston Quad, home to the first-year dorms and Brown's best dining hall, the Sharpe Refectory, better known as the Ratty. I haven't lived on campus for a few years but am feeling a little nostalgic thinking about graduating in six short weeks.

I'd picked Brown for the open curriculum where students choose their own education path, trying out different fields of study until they find their true passion. I'm on my way to earning an economics degree and have enjoyed four years of independence. Four years of freedom I desperately needed. They changed me. Brown's recruitment slogan pretty much sums up my life—"We live in a complex world, full of complex problems. How do we prepare the leaders of tomorrow?"

Strolling through the long shadow cast by Chapin, the on-campus football residence, I remember all the great things that happened during my time here as well as one terrible night. I shudder at the early April breeze and the memory of that night.

Like many seniors, I have the "What's going to happen now?" nervous anticipation of the unknown. Although my career path is already laid out—I'll be working for the Queen—I'm not entirely sure what will be expected of me or how much I'll have to sacrifice. Partial knowledge comes with its own kind of edgy anxiety.

My phone buzzes again. It's a text from Kat.

Kat: *You've been officially summoned by the Queen.*

Me: *So formal.* I joke back. The subtext of her message is that I've been away too long.

Not liking the thought of being ordered home, I call Kat to find out what's going on.

"You need to come home," Kat answers my call. She's all business today. Every day really.

"I'm preparing for finals, remember?"

"You need to come home right now," she repeats herself. "Something's happening."

"You'll send me back in a couple of hours though, right? My time here isn't done."

"I don't know, Nina." The call is heavy with what's not being said. "When you get here, go straight to court. The Queen is waiting for you."

I have an idea what this might be about. And if I've learned one thing during my time living Earthside, it's that I'll *never* allow anyone, including the Queen, to make decisions for me again.

"Will you be there?" I hold my breath hoping she'll be with me for moral support. The Queen can be . . . difficult.

"No, she wants to meet with you alone."

My stomach clenches at this unwelcome news.

Walking back into the shadow of Chapin, I tuck myself around the corner of the building. "I'm ready." I start shaking as Kat transfers enough power to me that I can jump out of the physical plane back to Avalon.

CHAPTER TWO

T HE TRIP BACK TO Avalon using Kat's power is almost instantaneous, my energy moving through time and space at the speed of light. Kat is a siren, and like others preternaturals who use sex and blood to fortify their magic—vampires, shifters and the fae, to name a few—she can jump between the planes. And she can lend her magic to others to do the same. Jumping between planes uses a lot of energy, and only the most powerful among us can do it.

Our existence is made up of several energy levels, or planes, similar to an atom. Earthside is at the center and the next plane up is inhabited by us. There are separate planes for each family of gods and goddesses—Egyptian, Norse, Roman and Greek, as well as the Titans. The outermost plane is occupied by the great beyond and the great darkness.

Avalon, an island country on the preternatural plane, is the seat of the Queen's power. All those who live on the island are invited guests of, work directly for or are aligned with the Queen in some way.

The Queen's stronghold on Avalon is an imposing limestone castle nestled on acres of green rolling land, with hills, dales, meadows and forests. Although the exterior appears medieval, the interior is plush, and all amenities are state of the art. While the entire castle is known as The Queen's Court, she does hold court in a large throne room. She is the law of the land and rules with an iron fist in a designer glove.

When I arrive in the castle, just outside her court, the large wooden double doors are closed and flanked by two members of the Gorm Guard. The Queen's personal guard is made up entirely of Gorm males. Their skin is various shades of blue and green arranged into intricate patterns that look like tattoos. Each Gorm's pattern and shading is unique, in the same way fingerprints are unique. Along with the appearance of their skin, their supernatural strength and thirst for violence are also hallmarks of their race. They're favorite hobby is going Earthside to look for ships to wreck and unsuspecting sailors to drown.

They lower their eyes to the floor when they see me, avoiding eye contact. It's not because I'm a snob or fear them and this is the way *I* want it. It's because this is the way *they* want it. The Gorm and I have a complicated history.

The Queen's chief secretary, Stewart, comes around his desk to greet me. "She's been waiting. I'll announce you."

"Court's quiet today, Stew."

"Yes, indeed. She's closed it."

"What do you mean? She never closes court. Do you know what's going on?"

Stewart shrugs his thin shoulders and sighs. "You know the Queen. She doesn't explain herself to anyone."

The guards move in unison to open the doors for the secretary, and he disappears behind them as they close.

I wait outside of court. And then wait some more. In ripped jeans, combat boots and an oversized sweater, I'm not exactly dressed to meet the Queen. I debate whether to risk her anger by being late because I went to my apartment to change or pissing her off with this outfit. I settle on the latter.

Almost an hour after he left me standing here, the doors open, and Stewart reappears. "She will see you now."

I pull back my shoulders and pass through the double doors. Walking across the black-and-white marble floors, I project a lot more confidence than I feel.

The Queen is right where I expect her to be—sitting on her red-velvet throne, looking down on the world from the raised dais flanked by Baroque-style columns. Her consort is seated in a smaller throne to her right. They're all decked out in ceremonial finery—including crowns and sashes—making me really regret not changing. And they're not alone.

A guy in a charcoal gray suit is standing right in front of the dais, talking quietly with them. He's tall and blond. Very tall, actually.

As I approach their little group, the Queen raises her chin and meets my eyes in greeting, "Good. You are here."

I've been here for an hour and have more important shit to do. I wisely keep that comment to myself and execute a perfect curtsy. "I'm here at your command. May I ask why?"

"I want to introduce you to someone. Or reintroduce is perhaps more accurate." The Queen motions to the guy in the gray suit. "Prince Ashton, the son and heir of Reginald Mountcastle, dragon shifter and controller of the Australias. Ashton, do you remember Princess Seraphina of Avalon, daughter of the Lady of the Lake? My daughter and heir."

I am her daughter, but the Queen hadn't raised me. There'd been no tea parties, story times or good-night hugs. While she'd been traveling across the planes performing her royal duties and managing her business interests, I'd grown up in the care of others. To me, she was the Queen first and my mother a very, very distant second.

"How could I forget Princess Seraphina?" He turns around and strolls toward me with loose-limbed confidence, giving me my first good look at him.

My eyes widen in shock. The memory of a young boy with white-blond hair, a dirty face and a split lip swims to the forefront of my mind. We'd visited his family's court a couple of times when I was young. On one trip, he'd put a snake down the bodice of my dress. We'd been a lot closer in size then, and I'd punched him in the face in retaliation. *Ah, the good old days.*

He takes my hand in a firm handshake. A jolt of awareness, like an electrical current, passes through me, but I hold on and strengthen my grip. And then he ever so slightly strengthens his.

He's much bigger and stronger than I am, so this is a pissing contest I probably can't win. But I also won't back down. What the hell is he even doing here? I made it perfectly clear to him that I'm not interested. Narrowing my eyes and gritting my teeth, I look up into his face and double down on the handshake. "Hello, Ash."

When neither one of us gives in and pulls away, the Queen intervenes. "You two are going to have to learn how to play nicely."

The consort seems particularly interested in the proceedings, staring down at us with an expectant expression on his smug face.

Ash releases my hand and gives me a knowing smile.

9

The Queen looks inexplicably pleased with herself.

All of a sudden, a sick feeling wells in my stomach. It's as if everyone is in on the joke but me.

"Princess Seraphina, meet your new betrothed." The Queen makes this announcement as if she's giving me a blue Tiffany box with a white satin ribbon on top.

"Well, we may have a little problem there. You see, I have some news of my own. I'm already engaged." Satisfaction blossoms in my chest as I watch the Queen's face harden.

CHAPTER THREE

"Yes, that's right, I'm engaged," I continue. "To Nicky. I mean Prince Nicola, son and heir of Franco Rossi, Master Vampire and Controller of Italy."

The Queen pins me with a dark stare. "No, you are not. I did not accept Nicola's marriage contract. As a matter of fact, I rejected it and sent it back to him just before you arrived. You never had my approval to marry Nicola."

I don't look at Ash. My eyes are entirely for the Queen. "I need to speak with you. Alone." The fact that she rejected Nicky's contract almost brings me to my knees, but I'm not giving up. I need to talk her out of this decision.

She doesn't acknowledge me because no one commands the Queen. No one.

Instead, she says, "Ashton has asked for your hand in marriage, and I have accepted. A new marriage contract has been drawn up. It is with your lawyer."

I need to slow this down and get the Queen to see reason. "May I please speak with you alone?" I ask the Queen.

"Make an appointment with Stewart for tomorrow morning."

"I wasn't planning on staying the night. I was planning to go right back to school." I do some deep breathing exercises.

"Your plans have changed." She dismisses me with a wave.

"May I speak, Your Majesty?" Ash breaks in.

"Permission granted."

"I'd like to formally request a change to the contract." Ash turns to me. "Specifically, I'd like to change the length of the betrothal from six months to one week. I no longer want a long engagement."

"One week? That's ridiculous! I'm still in school. I don't graduate for over a month," I shout.

The Queen holds up a silencing hand. "Do you have a reason for making this request, Ashton? What you want is not a particular concern of this court."

Finally, some straight talk.

Ash continues, "You've accepted my binding contract, so I see no reason to delay. And after seeing the princess in person, I realize something I've long suspected. She's my fated mate."

Binding, mate, mated—those terms are more commonly used in a shifter court, while wedding, husband, wife, marriage—are more commonly used in mine. And this fated mate business, recognizing your one true love through some kind of instinct, is shifter folklore. I don't even think it's real.

"Your fated mate? That is a bold statement. Are you sure?" the Queen asks.

"Yes," he answers confidently.

"If you are worried that I will change my mind and rescind acceptance, you need not worry." The Queen's arched brow lets Ash know she doesn't like her honor being questioned.

"I certainly wasn't implying you'd go back on your word, Your Majesty. I simply want to move forward. Why postpone the inevitable?" Ash's low bow makes me want to gag.

The Queen sits in contemplative silence for a moment. "I will allow Ashton's change to the contract. The wedding ceremony will take place one week from today."

What the fuck is happening? I'm speechless.

Ash turns to me and smiles in victory. "As a show of good faith, I think we should allow the princess to negotiate a clause as well."

"How very generous of you." I infuse sarcasm into every word. I'm shaking all over and hoping he doesn't notice. Who does this overgrown *lizard* think he is? Telling me how things are going to work in *my* mother's court. *My* future court.

The Queen sits back in her throne and wrinkles her nose, looking less than thrilled with this concession for me. "Very well. I agree. We will give the princess some time to recover herself and decide on the clause she would like to negotiate. We will reconvene tomorrow afternoon. Ashton, the guards will show you to your rooms."

"Hand me your phone." Ash unlocks his and passes it to me. Without thinking, I take it and hand him mine, unlocked. Our phones instantly change color, indicating they're no longer with their owner. Ash's changes from graphite blue to white and mine from platinum to hot pink.

We use phones similar to those available Earthside, but many generations more advanced. All technology is developed on a higher plane and then delivered Earthside. My world is a dichotomy between great technological advancement and rigid adherence to the etiquette and tradition of a royal monarchy.

"Give me your number. Your *new* one." He sounds as if he's giving directions to a toddler. He types his number into my phone manually. If he were using his own phone, he'd enter the information using biomechanics. Once synced with your body's biology and muscular activity, you can perform tasks on your phone using small movements of your muscles.

I seriously think about giving him a fake number. But that would be petty. Not that I'm above being petty. It just wouldn't serve a purpose in this instance. I type in my real number. "We could have just airdropped each other our contact info."

"I wasn't sure you'd accept mine. Just want to make sure you have it." Ash looks down on me with an air of superiority.

After we exchange phones, Ash bows to the Queen and consort and backs out of court, never once raising his eyes or turning his back to the Queen. He knows the unwritten rules. Even an imagined slight to the Queen would see him tossed out on his ear. Or worse. His manners are perfect.

I open my mouth to speak, but before anything can come out, the Queen cuts me off. "You are excused. I suggest you settle in. Get reacquainted with your life."

CHAPTER FOUR

I BOW MY HEAD and back from the room. As soon as I'm out of the Queen's sight, I straighten up and march down the hall. Two members of the Gorm Guard follow me, keeping a respectful distance.

I call Nicky. No answer.

I text him: *I'm so sorry she rejected your contract. Please call me.* If I think too much about what just happened in court, my heart will break, so I cling to my anger instead.

Walking to my apartment, I think about how Nicky had appeared in my life one day. On a whim and because I needed an art elective to graduate, I'd enrolled in a drawing and painting night class. I was terrible at it. And although the prof never said anything, I could tell he wondered what the hell I was doing there. But you can't fail art, right?

One night, I walked into art class, and there was a gorgeous brown-haired, brown-eyed guy sitting on the edge of the prof's desk. We made direct eye contact, and our gazes held.

When I was able to pull my eyes away from his and make my way to my seat, I was in a brain fog, and my body was covered in goosebumps.

He introduced himself to the class as Nicola "Nicky" Rossi, the guest professor for the rest of the semester.

I knew who he was right away. His paintings and sculptures are exhibited in the best galleries and museums, and he has a massive social following. He's also a vampire from an influential royal family. Not as influential as mine, but few are. Royal circles are small, and you tend to know of someone even if you haven't met them.

Nicky made his way around the room, examining everyone's work. When he finally made it to me and looked at my painting, he asked, not unkindly, "Are you a science major?"

"No, economics," I replied, my heart pounding at his nearness.

He bit his lower lip and continued to stare at my painting. Finally, he said, "Your lines are very straight. I can see I'm going to have to teach you how to color outside them."

As I walked out at the end of class, he stopped me and handed me a slip of paper. "Bella, here's my address. Come over tonight. Around eleven."

Normally, I don't go out with random guys I just met, but I couldn't resist him. There was something about him. Saying no wasn't an option.

When I arrived at his house that night, a gracious Victorian just off campus, he invited me in and led me to his studio, where he announced, "We're going to paint!"

He sat me down on the floor, which was covered by drop cloths, in front of a large blank canvas. Then he put several cans of paint in front of me and a selection of brushes in different sizes and shapes.

"Let's have some fun," he said as he sat behind me, his hard body surrounding mine. Picking up a brush, he dipped it in a can and flicked his wrist so the paint hit the canvas. "There's no right or wrong here. Do whatever you feel. Go ahead."

My whole life, I'd been afraid of doing or saying the wrong thing. Making a mistake. Disappointing the Queen. I was like a prisoner being set free after a long incarceration. I didn't know what to do with my freedom and sat there immobilized. Seeing my struggle, he grabbed a brush, put it in my right hand and then dipped the brush into a can of paint. He flicked my hand so the paint hit the canvas. "Stop thinking, Bella." He laughed quietly.

We took turns flicking paint at the canvas, laughing and talking. I felt accepted for who I was. There was no pressure to be anyone else; no expectations. It was liberating.

That's how our whirlwind romance started and I was instantly obsessed with him.

When I reach my apartment, I burst through the doors, too furious to be soothed by the decor of white and cream, the plush furniture or the large windows displaying scenic garden views. The guards close the doors and stand outside them.

A bit of movement catches my eye, and I have almost no time to react before two large dogs come barreling toward me. Falling to my knees, I open my arms wide and welcome my two hellhounds, Steel and Silver. "Hello, boys. Hello! Who's so handsome? Who's a good boy? I know, I haven't seen you in months. I'm sorry. It's been too long." Not having seen me since Christmas break, they knock me over in their excitement. I sit on the floor, petting and hugging them as they yip in happiness and rub up against me, tails wagging. Playing with my dogs centers me, cooling my anger somewhat.

Arranged marriages are not unheard of in royal circles. The system was originally developed as a way to unite and maintain the stability of powerful monarchies. Instead of love, arranged marriages are based on a mutual understanding between the families. But the Queen had never hinted that I would have one. We'd never even discussed it. I'd assumed, obviously incorrectly, that I'd get to choose my own husband. Create my own marriage contract. *Has everyone lost their minds while I've been away at school?*

After a quick *tap tap*, the door to my apartment flies open. "And the prodigal daughter returns. Welcome home. You've walked into a shit show." Katherine—Kat—is not only one of my best friends, but my hard-nosed lawyer, too.

I stand up and give my hellhounds a few more scratches behind the ears before Kat gives me a quick one-armed squeeze. She's normally not one for displays of affection, so the fact that she hugs me, albeit quickly, indicates how bad this is.

"Where's Sofie and Gia?" I ask.

"They're on their way. It's all hands on deck." Kat settles on the plush white sectional and opens her laptop. I curl up in the corner closest to her.

Sophia is my private physician; a real tender-hearted motherly-type. Georgia is my fun-loving publicist and social media manager. And, like Kat, they're sirens. The three of them split their time between being Earthside with me and here on Avalon. They're also leaders in their chosen fields and often guest lecture at Earthside colleges and universities.

The four of us have been best friends since the Queen took them into her court and protected them. Their race was almost hunted to extinction by other preternaturals who believed drinking siren blood was some kind of immortality elixir. In return for sanctuary, they promised the Queen to safeguard and nurture me for as long as I needed them.

It's unusual for sirens to act as caregivers or protectors, but their ability to alter their appearance and their power of telepathy to perceive what others need them to be make them particularly good at the role.

Despite being gods knows how old, they always appear to be the same age as me. We'd gone through childhood and the awkward adolescent stage together. Now that I'm an adult and require a staff, they evolved to fill those roles. *I can't imagine my life without them.*

Without knocking, Gia and Sofie walk in, bringing me back to the present. Their faces are creased with worry. I stand up from the couch and walk into Sofie's outstretched arms. She wraps her arms firmly around me and gives me a long hug. When Sofie and I part, Gia throws her arms loosely around my neck and gives me a smacking kiss on the cheek. Then we all join Kat on the couch, the dogs lying down on the floor in front of us.

"I have some stuff to tell you all," I say, looking at each of my besties in turn. "But Kat, can you please start at the beginning and tell me what the hell is going on here?"

"Right after the Queen asked me to summon you"—Kat's brow furrows—"she informed me she had disallowed the marriage contract from Nicky. That Ashton Mountcastle had asked for permission to marry you and that she had granted it. Her lawyers sent over the new contract, and I've been looking it over. I forwarded a copy to Sofie and Gia, and they've reviewed it, too." Kat opens her laptop and looks at the screen. "Apparently, he delivered the contract in person, and he's here in the castle."

The creation of a marriage contract is standard practice for all royal weddings, arranged or not, and takes a lot of work. Royal families don't like surprises. Each side undergoes medical testing and fills out questionnaire after questionnaire. The questions range from "What's your favorite color?" to "How many partners have you had penetrative sexual intercourse with?" And everything in between.

"Was he there when you met with the Queen? What's he like?" Gia's eyebrows rise over her bright eyes. She leans in, resting her chin on her closed fist.

"He's an arrogant ass." I describe Ash perfectly in four words.

"Well, he looks good on paper. Six foot five. Two hundred and twenty pounds," Kat says.

"He's a big oaf," I say quickly. "No, make that a troll. And not the internet kind. The kind that lives under bridges and eats human flesh."

Kat ignores me and continues. "Blond hair, hazel eyes."

"More like dirty blond. And his eyes are so beady I couldn't really tell the color." With a wave of my hand, I dismiss Ash's looks entirely.

"He's twenty-five, and it looks like he's got a birthday coming up this month." Kat scrolls down her laptop screen.

"Ugh, that makes him a Taurus. The worst sign." I shake my head at another strike against Ash.

Kat rolls her eyes at me. "How is Taurus the worst sign?"

"First of all, everyone knows Gemini is the worst sign," Gia pipes up. "And really, Nina, you're a Scorpio. A Taurus *could* be a good match for you. You'll either have a long passionate marriage, or you'll kill each other within a week. Could go either way."

Kat gets us back on topic. "Never mind his sign. Let's move on. His father is a dragon shifter, and his mother is a green witch."

"As a green witch, she has the ability to draw energy from the natural world, and is well known for her skills in creating healing potions from plants, flowers and herbs. That makes

Ash a dragon shifter with a little extra juice from his mother's side." Sofie is our resident expert on all things related to power.

"His mother's name is Marigold. How pretty is that?" Gia smiles. Of all of us, she's the one who always tries to find the bright side.

Kat gives me a sympathetic look. "Ashton's power rating is *Very High*. No surprise there. His parents are powerful."

"Great," I grit out. Power is a sore subject with me. I don't have mine yet, and no one can explain why.

Kat smirks. "Oh, this is interesting. He's the oldest of four siblings. That's a lot of kids. He comes from a prolific bloodline."

"Ash's fertility rating is *Excellent*," Sofie says in her doctor voice. "All of his sperm tests—semen volume, sperm number, vitality, motility, shape—all *Excellent*."

"Sounds like his boys are good swimmers." Gia giggles.

"Oh, my gods! I don't want to talk about his sperm." I don't need to ask about my ratings. My power is *TBD*, and my fertility is graded as *Fair*. "He looks like a fucking thoroughbred, and I look like a half-lame donkey. But maybe my lackluster ratings can work in my favor. After all, what prince wants a powerless, infertile princess?"

"Yeah, and he has more followers on social than you, too."
Gia adds insult to injury.

Since coming out to the humans, we've enjoyed celebrity
status, with social media followers outnumbering the
Kardashians. Humans have an insatiable appetite for seeing
how the other half lives. And like their fascination with the
super wealthy of their own species, humans are endlessly
fascinated by us. They are drawn to our magic, our
otherness. They can't help but watch our every move with
voyeuristic obsession.

Humans have suspected, but never had proof, that we
existed until the Rampages hit ten years ago. The Rampages
were a series of pathogens released Earthside that killed
millions of humans. No one is sure where the pathogens
came from—some think they were human-made population
control experiments; others believe they came from a
misbehaving god who wanted to stir up trouble and watch
the misery. To restore order, our scientists developed
an antidote and then sent a carefully selected team of
ambassadors to deliver it to the humans. One of those
ambassadors was the Queen.

The pathogens mutated several times, and each time we
provided a new antidote. The humans were so grateful for
the aid and so exhausted by the Rampages they were fine
with our coming out and walking among them. More than
fine; they embraced us with open arms.

So we entwined ourselves with the human experience, and before long, it felt as if we'd always been there. And in a way we had—the humans just hadn't known it. It's startling what humans can get used to in a relatively short period of time.

"Which apps does he have more followers on, Gia?" My eyes narrow in irritation.

"All of them. I'm always telling you to post some bikini pics. Some lingerie shots." Gia gives me an "I told you so" look.

"The Queen would *love* that." I snort. "Does Ash have a copy of my info already?"

"Yes, it would've been added to his contract," Kat assures me.

"Fuck this whole marriage contract business." My anger returns to full boil. "Going through all these tests. Writing all this stuff down so some shithead lawyers can pour over it and point out all my faults. No offense, Kat."

"None taken." Kat gives me a wry smile.

"I went through all of this for Nicky. I never for a second thought the Queen would hijack my info and use it to create another contract for an arranged marriage I don't want. It's bad enough she's preventing me from marrying Nicky, but forcing me to marry Ash is next level. The Queen never gave me any indication she was going to arrange a marriage for me. We didn't have one conversation."

"She doesn't explain herself to anyone. But this does seem particularly underhanded. Even for the Queen." Kat nods solemnly.

"And speaking of shitheads, Ash starts talking about some fated-mate shifter bullshit and then asked the Queen to shorten the engagement from six months to a week. *A week!* And she agreed!" As I fill them in on what happened at court, my rage has me practically levitating off the couch. "Not only that, he's *allowing me* to change a clause in the contract, too. *Allowing me* as a sign of good faith. Can you believe this guy?"

"Do you know which clause you want to change?" Kat grabs the top right and bottom left corners of her laptop screen and pulls diagonally to stretch it, then flips her enlarged screen around so I can see the contract.

I look at her as if she has three heads. Why is she talking about this as if it's a foregone conclusion? "I don't want to change a clause. I want to find a way out of this. I have to change the Queen's mind."

"The contract appears to be in order. It's legal and binding. No pun intended. The Queen is within her rights to choose a husband for you, Nina." Kat is in full-on lawyer mode now.

The Queen may have blindsided me by accepting Ash's marriage contract, but I'm far from throwing in the towel. During our meeting tomorrow, I'll present my case; make her understand that a marriage to Ashton Mountcastle is simply not going to happen.

CHAPTER FIVE

T HE NEXT MORNING FINDS me standing in the antechamber of the Queen's office. In a short-sleeve, knee-length navy-blue dress patterned with tiny white flowers and tan espadrilles, I look as though I'm heading out to meet friends for a fun day of shopping and lunch. Instead, I'm going to battle the Queen.

Stewart shows me into her sparse office where wainscoting and coffered ceilings are the only decoration. There are no personal mementos or framed pictures—even of me; her only child.

She's working behind a large wooden desk, not a hair out of place and wearing a vintage Chanel suit and the dark-rimmed glasses she wears for effect. Like Coco, she's polished the look with a set of pearls. These pearls had been harvested and gifted to her by Poseidon himself. Nothing but the best for the Queen.

I may have gotten my looks from her—long brown hair, full lips and gray tip-tilted eyes—but that's where the similarities end.

The Queen is a force of nature, and power radiates off her. She comes from a long line of enchantresses—those who are able to manipulate energy—and she's the most powerful one of all. Our family line sprung from the combined magic of a witch and a fae. From a relationship that started in love and ended in violence.

As soon as I sit in the chair opposite her desk, her power rolls over my skin like water. And just like water, I'm aware of it, but it isn't hurting me. For now.

The Queen tilts her head to the side and regards me. "Princess Seraphina, how are you?"

Here we go. That question is code for "Any sign of your power?" My mother is like a dog with a bone. "I'm fine. Thank you." My answer to the unspoken question is no.

She looks at me blankly, as if she has no idea why I'm sitting in her office this morning. Her motto is: Never Complain. Never Explain.

But I'm here for an explanation. I clear my throat. "I wanted to talk to you about yesterday. About what happened at court." Her power is still a pleasant sensation, but I'm not fooled. I've been down this road before. First, she lulls you into a state of relaxation, creating a false sense of security, and then she goes in for the kill.

"Yes?" She lifts her eyes and waits for me to continue. She's not going to make this easy on me.

"Why are you doing this? Why are you preventing me from marrying the guy I want and forcing me into a marriage with someone who is basically a stranger?" I can't believe I have to spell it out for her.

She sits back and takes off her glasses. "Imagine my surprise when Nicola Rossi's offer of marriage came across my desk. You have never mentioned him to me. Not once. You are my sole heir and knew I would want to be informed about this kind of alliance. And yet you went ahead and arranged a marriage with Nicola behind my back. Why the secrecy?"

"It wasn't a secret. I just wanted everything to be in order for you to review. I thought formal was the best route to take. Dotting the i's, crossing the t's." I work hard at keeping my face as blank as hers, my voice smooth and confident.

If her frown and pursed lips are any indication, she isn't buying what I'm selling. "Be that as it may, a marriage to him, aligning with the Rossi family, would do nothing to ensure the future of this court. If you had consulted me beforehand, I could have saved you and Nicola the embarrassment of rejecting his contract. Nicola is not the right match for you."

"How do you know? You've never even met him." The temperature and pressure of her magic rises slightly, making the air humid and uncomfortable to breathe.

"I know his type. He is a brilliant artist and very pretty to look at, but he is not for you. His work is his passion, and that will never change. You, this court, our businesses, would never be his first priority. He might have played at it for a few years. But eventually, he would have gone back to what he loves, his art. Also, vampires are not known for being the best breeders, and you need all the help you can get in that department."

Ouch. "I know you only care about this court, but just because he won't be working in it, doesn't mean he doesn't offer anything of value. Nicky and I care about each other. Doesn't that count for anything?" My breath is coming fast and shallow. I'm not sure whether it's a reaction to her power, or the uncompromising expression on her face.

"Does he care about you? Are you sure about that? The Rossi family is well known for their greed, unsavory business dealings and empire-building. There are rumors circulating that his father, Franco, may be trying to take over more Earthside territory. They will have to use force to accomplish that. And you, my dear, come from a particularly powerful family, even if you do not have any magic of your own. I have no interest in aligning my power with the Rossis."

Is it so hard to believe Nicky could want me just for me? I blink several times and try to steady my breathing. It's all about alliances and political power with the Queen. What she fails to realize is that Nicky couldn't care less about those things. He isn't active in his father's court and doesn't care about strengthening his family's empire. And the fact that his art is his first priority is not a downside to me. It's one of the things that drew me to him in the first place. He's built an exciting life of his own, outside of the traditional royal constraints of duty and responsibility.

"My mind is made up. You will marry Ashton. He comes from a respected, influential family and is powerful in his own right. He can protect you until your power arrives, *if it ever does.* You know there have been threats against me. An assassination attempt. What if something happened to me tomorrow? I have to prepare you and this court for the future." She rubs the furrows from her forehead before continuing. "You have a life of privilege, Seraphina, but privilege is not free. It comes with sacrifice. You had your years of fun at school, but now you have to take on your responsibilities." Her eyes are cold and her flat tone allows no room for argument.

"I'm prepared to take on my responsibilities where this court is concerned. And step up to do my duty as your successor. But I don't need an arranged marriage with Ashton Mountcastle to do it. What do we really know about him anyway?" The heat and force of her energy continues to increase. If she keeps this up, I'll soon be boiled alive or crushed to death.

"I have known the Mountcastles for years, and an alliance with them will help ensure the long-term security of this court." She sighs and checks the time on her phone, signaling she's bored by me and this entire conversation. "Ashton believes you are his fated mate. He will put you and this court first. He offers stability that Nicola does not."

"I don't believe in this fated-mate business. It's just a shifter fairy tale as far as I'm concerned. And even if it's true, Ash could be lying. Wouldn't I know if I was his fated mate. I feel nothing for him."

She shakes her head, disregarding my concerns. "Successful arranged marriages between royal families have been happening since time immemorial. Think of it as a business deal if you wish. A merger between two powerful families with like-minded interests. That should appeal to your economist's brain." She pauses, her eyes taking on a merciless gleam. "Your playtime at school is over. Your life as you knew it is gone."

"I'm only a few weeks from graduating!" I've put in four years of overcaffeinated all-nighters and have a permanently reserved table at the library.

"Your place is here now. You will turn all your time and attention to your union with Ashton. You will fulfill your obligations to Avalon. That is an order."

Just then, Stewart enters the office and stands silently inside the open door, indicating my time is up.

Going head-to-head with her is not my way forward. I need to go head-to-head with Ash. "As the Queen commands it, so shall it be done." I recite the familiar mantra, infusing my voice with only a hint of the bitterness and contempt I feel.

After leaving the Queen, I head back to my apartment and cuddle up on the couch with Steel and Silver. I try calling Nicky again. And again. And again. No answer.

So I send him another text: *We need to talk. Please call me back. I'm so sorry.*

I've been trying to reach him ever since I returned to Avalon with no success. I hope he's just working and hasn't given up on us. Tossing my phone aside, I give each of the dogs a scratch behind the ears, taking comfort in their quiet company.

How is it possible that so much has changed so quickly? One minute, I'm happily engaged to Nicky and have so much to look forward to. The next, I'm betrothed to Ash.

I need some time to figure out how to break Ash's contract and get my life back on track. Running my fingers through the fur on the back of Silver's neck, I'm struck by a flash of inspiration. "I have an idea," I say aloud and watch Steel and Silver's ears perk up. Smiling, I pick up my phone to call Kat.

CHAPTER SIX

I MAY HAVE LOST the battle with the Queen, but I still plan to win the war. No matter what, I'm going back to school and going back to Nicky.

Sweeping into the Queen's court later that afternoon wearing a cropped gray pantsuit, I mean business. Kat, in a black pencil skirt and blazer, is by my side.

We stand in front of the Queen and her consort. The consort, although married to the Queen, is not her co-ruler. He's her adviser, and as a fae, does have his own power, but he doesn't have the title or role of King. He's also not my father, and has never tried to play the role.

My father died shortly after I was born, and I don't remember him at all. There is one large painting of him in one of the smaller sitting rooms, but there are no other pictures of my father in the castle. Perhaps it's to spare the consort's feelings. No one likes to be reminded of the ex.

Kat and I curtsy to the Queen and the consort, and then as a unified force, we turn and regard Ash and the guy standing beside him, who must be his lawyer.

The Queen opens the proceedings. "We're here to allow Princess Seraphina to negotiate a clause in her marriage contract with Ashton Mountcastle. Princess, have you selected the clause you wish to negotiate?"

"Section 5.1.6, paragraph B," Kat responds on my behalf, adjusting her glasses. "That's the consummation date, my Queen. Currently, it's within six hours of the wedding ceremony or binding as some call it." She nods briskly to Ash and his lawyer. "We'd like to change it to one year from the ceremony."

"Permission to speak, Your Majesty?" Ashton's lawyer immediately interjects. He's wearing a dark blue suit over his tall, wiry frame.

"Granted," the Queen graciously replies, her eyes flashing with interest.

"With all due respect to the princess"—he nods his head courteously toward me—"that's not going to work. She needs to choose a more reasonable time frame. We suggest twenty-four hours."

"Twenty-four hours!" I level a steely glare at Ash. "What kind of bad faith negotiation is this? You've shortened the engagement to a mere week, and now you want the consummation to happen right away? We don't even know each other. I need more time." I should be conferring with Kat and allowing her to do the talking, but I can't stop myself from going toe-to-toe with Ash.

Ash's broad shoulders are relaxed and he speaks calmly and quietly. "I had legitimate reasons for requesting a shortened engagement. First of all, the Queen has already accepted my contract. And second, I'm claiming you as my fated mate. There is absolutely no reason to hold off on consummating the binding for a year." He raises a single eyebrow at me. "Not to mention, I'm contractually obligated to get you pregnant. That's going to be difficult to do if we're not sleeping together. I offered you the right to negotiate terms as a courtesy. You're making me wish I hadn't. I'll wait a week."

"Nine months," I counter, hoping I sound as in control as he does.

"Two weeks." He has the audacity to look at the Queen. "This is a deal breaker."

Everyone in the room knows the underlying subtext here. Just like Earthside, until a wedding ceremony is consummated, sealed by sex, we won't be legally married. We'll be in a state of limbo. The marriage can be annulled. As if it never happened. It's a stall tactic on my part, and a pretty desperate one at that. But it's all I have.

"I accept that we're going to be married," I say, bowing my head to Ash in a fake show of submission. "I just think we need some time to get to know each other is all." Raising my head, I meet his gaze with my biggest, softest doe eyes.

Ash maintains our eye contact. "Fine, one month. That's it. Don't press this point further, or I'll ask my lawyer to research if there is any precedence for negotiating this clause at all. And *Princess*, you don't leave Avalon until this binding is consummated." He uses my title as a mocking nickname.

A month is not a lot of time to find a way out of this mess. But it's a long time to be away from Nicky. It's also a long time to be out of school leading up to finals and graduation. *Fuck.*

"Ashton, you've been more generous than expected with Princess Seraphina," the Queen announces. A meaningful look passes between them before she gives Ash a tight smile.

I'm not sure what that look means, but I don't like it. The Queen has no smile for me. Huge surprise.

Kat stands in front of me and speaks directly to Ash's lawyer, "Amend the paperwork and send it to us. We'll need a chance to review."

"We want it signed today," the other lawyer replies matter-of-factly.

"If it's in good order, our side will sign," Kat retorts.

The Queen settles more comfortably on her throne and folds her hands in her lap. "This is cause for celebration. I will host a dinner tomorrow night to toast the newly betrothed couple. Stewart will text the details."

Three hours later a hard copy of the contract is delivered to my apartment by royal messenger and a digital copy arrives with a ping in Kat's inbox. Marriage contracts require wet signatures. I wish I was signing in Ash's blood.

Kat opens the packet and holds up the contract so I can see the Queen's seal on the front. "It has royal approval," she says with finality. We both know my signature is merely a formality at this point. She flips through the pages and finds the two changed clauses. Ash's change to the length of the betrothal and my change to the consummation date. His and hers. "These look correct. I'm going to take this back to my office and give it one more thorough read through. Make sure those fuckers haven't changed anything else. Tried to slip something by us."

"Thank you, Kat." I give her a sad smile, suddenly feeling wiped out. I didn't sleep much last night, staring at my phone, praying Nicky would return my messages. Lying down on the couch, I pull a faux white fur throw over my body, close my eyes and fall into a restless sleep.

I dream of being chased down a long, dark hallway. The sensation of being prey consumes me with a soul-deep dread. Looking back over my shoulder in a state of near hysteria, I try to see who's chasing me, but can only make out a vague silhouette. Even so, I know it's a male. I also know with heart-pounding certainty that he's gaining on me and that if he catches me, I'll never be the same. Running as fast as I can down the narrow hall, I feel his sinister presence only a few feet behind me right before he grabs my shoulder in a bruising grip.

My eyes fly open and I bolt upright.

Kat is standing over me. "Nina, sorry to wake you. But it's all in order. No funny business."

"This whole situation is funny business," I say, catching my breath and shrugging off the lingering fear from the dream. "This should be Nicky's marriage contract I'm signing, not Ash's." Pushing off the throw and planting my feet on the floor, I hold out my hand for the pen I'll use to sign my life away.

Kat sits beside me and has me initial the bottom right corner of every page, right beside where Ash had done the same. The sight of his initials enrages me. When that is done, Kat reopens the document to the first updated clause. I read it and then initial and date beside it to indicate I acknowledge the change. Kat flips through the pages again and points to the second update. I read it, and again initial and date the change. Then she flips to the last page.

I look at Ash's signature where Nicky's should be, and all of a sudden it becomes very real and a sense of impending doom overtakes me. I am going to be married to someone I don't know and don't want. "I need to get out of this, Kat," I whisper urgently. "I have to find a way." With an unsteady hand, I sign.

CHAPTER SEVEN

T RUE TO HER WORD, the Queen arranges a dinner party the following night. The guest list is small: she and the consort, my girls and I, Ash and a few members of his entourage. Royalty never travels light.

The girls and I are the last to enter the dining room the Queen uses for small gatherings. The warm glow from the Murano glass chandelier twinkles off the glassware on the lavishly set table, creating an intimate atmosphere.

I took extra time getting ready this evening. I want to knock Ash dead and then step over his lifeless body. My long hair falls straight down my back, and my little black dress is a figure-skimming, strapless number with a slit on the right thigh. A pair of strappy black heels and a velvet choker complete my outfit. The girls are similarly styled in cocktail dresses with Kat in red, her sable hair pulled back in a low-slung ponytail; Sofie in teal, blond hair in a loose updo, and Gia in silver sequins, her gorgeous red hair not needing any color competition.

When the girls and I enter the dining room, a waiter greets us with a tray of chilled champagne flutes. After we each take a glass of champagne, I lift mine and murmur so only the girls can hear me, "This is going to be an awkward evening. Liquid courage is a must." Then we all raise our glasses slightly in a sign of solidarity before taking a sip.

Standing toward the head of the table, the Queen and the consort have their heads together, deep in conversation. As usual, the consort doesn't acknowledge me and keeps his face turned to the Queen. He's using his fae glamor to bend the light around him so he appears nondescript and fades into the background. I think he does this so the Queen can shine brighter.

She lifts her eyes to the girls and me in acknowledgment, and we each lower ours in deference and dip a small curtsy. She then turns back to the consort, and they resume their conversation, most likely talking about a real estate deal Earthside or something happening at court. To me, they seem much more like business partners than a couple. There is never any PDA. No touching at all actually. No lingering looks or flirtatious glances. They never raise their voices. They're always perfectly polite to each other. They don't generate enough spark to light a candle on a cupcake.

Ash, wearing a dark suit, white shirt and silver tie, saunters confidently across the dining room to greet us. I don't want to watch him, but I can't help it. He has that quality where you can't take your eyes off him. For a moment, I find myself wondering what he looks like under that suit.

"Princess, you look lovely." He takes my elbow and kisses me lightly on the cheek. "Introduce me to your friends."

The feel of his lips on my cheek flusters me until I remember how he's crashed into my life and changed all my plans. My anger comes charging back, and the temptation to toss my glass of champagne into his arrogant face is almost overwhelming. But I can feel the Queen's hawk eyes on me from across the room, watching me for any sign of rebellion. So, I resist the urge and introduce each of the sirens to him and his entourage, who have come to join our circle.

When I finish, he turns to his group. "This is Lucas Blackstone and Maximilian Hart. Luke is my lawyer, who I'm sure you recognize, and Max is my personal physician. And this is Bennet, Ben, my little brother."

There are handshakes and hellos all around. It's all *sooooo* civilized.

And then Ben addresses the elephant in the room. "Nina, I can't believe you and my brother are getting hitched. Basically, sight unseen." Ben is shorter than Ash and a bit stockier with a boyishly handsome face and a devilish smile. Apparently, blond hair runs in the Mountcastle family, but Ben's eyes are brown.

"Ben, I can honestly say, no one is more shocked than me."
I give Ash some serious side-eye.

The dining room doors open, and waiters file in carrying
covered plates. "Dinner is served," the lead waiter
announces.

Ash lifts his eyebrows at his brother in a look that seems to
say "Shut the fuck up."

Ben slides his hands in his pockets and smiles back at Ash.

We move as a group to the long table and turn over
delicate place cards to find our assigned seats. Surprise,
surprise—Ash and I are seated right beside each other. He
pulls out the upholstered chair for me. I guess he isn't a total
Neanderthal. As I take my seat, his fingers brush my arm, and
heat immediately rushes through me. I take a deep breath
and get a hold of myself.

We eat the first few courses in tense silence. I'm careful not
to accidentally bump elbows with Ash, wanting to avoid any
further physical contact. And I pointedly brush aside all of
his attempts at small talk.

When the third course plates are placed before us and the
silver cloches removed, Ash looks from his plate to mine.
Back to his. "Why does your lobster look different than
mine?"

"The Queen prefers warm water lobster from the lagoons at the base of Mount Olympus, and that's what she serves at parties. I like cold water lobster from Earthside, preferably from Nova Scotia or Maine."

"Do you hear yourself? Talk about first world problems." Ash shakes his head at me.

"What? I'm not allowed to have likes and dislikes?" Why does his every word irritate the ever-loving fuck out of me? I take my earlier assessment back. He *is* a total Neanderthal.

"Okay, tell me what makes cold water lobster so much better then." He grins at me, ignoring my scowl.

That grin incites a riot of butterflies in my stomach that I stomp down without mercy. I refuse to like him. My heart belongs to Nicky. "The meat is much sweeter and has a better texture." I stop the fork midway to my mouth to show off the firm, white flesh of the tail.

"Mind if I give it a try?" Ash places a large, warm hand over mine, and the butterflies are back in full force.

I watch in bewitched fascination as he guides the fork to his mouth, never letting go of my hand. It's shockingly intimate. I watch as his lips part, and he glides the fork into his mouth . . . a mouth I suddenly find mesmerizing. I give my head a shake and yank my hand back, breaking the spell.

Ash continues to eat as if nothing has passed between us. He uses my fork to take a bite of the lobster from his plate. Then, taking a second bite of mine, he chews slowly as if weighing a big decision.

"Apologies, Princess. You're right. Yours is better. Way better. Here, try some." He uses my fork to spear a piece of the seafood and holds it up to my mouth. A taunting gleam in his eye.

"I'm perfectly capable of feeding myself. *Thank you.*" I keep my eyes straight ahead and ignore his offering.

"Do it, Princess. Open your mouth and take it."

The double entendre is not lost on me, and I squeeze my thighs together under the table in response.

"You're making a scene. People are beginning to stare," Ash scolds.

"I'm making a scene? Really? Oh fine. Someone has to be the adult." I eat the bite of lobster.

Ash gives me a satisfied smirk. "I knew it wouldn't be long before I had you eating out of the palm of my hand."

"You're not deathly allergic to shellfish by any chance, are you?" I ask sweetly.

"Afraid not," he chuckles.

POWER HUNGRY

"You can't blame a girl for hoping."

CHAPTER EIGHT

T HE NEXT MORNING, ASH texts and asks me to meet him. For a split second, I think about ignoring him but then show the text to Kat.

"Keep your friends close and your enemies closer." Kat's toothy smile doesn't reach her eyes, reminding me of a shark. Kat and the girls are very protective of me. Always have been.

When I was six years old, a member of the Gorm Guard reached up under my dress and touched me where no adult should touch a child. I was so young, I didn't understand what was happening. When I told the girls what the guard had done, they'd ripped him to pieces using nothing but their teeth and nails, leaving a shredded pile of bloody gore behind. That's when the Gorm started lowering their eyes in apology whenever they saw me.

Then, during my first week at Brown, I'd been sexually assaulted by a frat boy as I walked home alone from a freshman orientation party. I'll never forget the sick, helpless feeling of being overpowered, his hands on my body without my permission. But he got more than he bargained for when he dragged me into the bushes and tried to rape me. Kat found us as he was ripping my pants off, and she snapped his neck, killing him instantly. Then she dumped his body in Chapin, the on-campus football dorm, making it look like an unfortunate accident—he'd had too much to drink and had fallen down the stairs. The only regret I have about his death is that Kat killed him too quickly.

I text Ash back: W*hat apartment are you in?*

He answers: *Atlantica*.

An hour later, I'm knocking on his door.

When he opens the door, my breath hitches involuntarily as I'm struck by how good looking he is. His almond-shaped hazel eyes shine with intelligence; his nose is bold and straight over full lips and a strong chin. The old saying is true: the whole is greater than the sum of its parts. His T-shirt stretches across his broad shoulders and muscular chest. His jeans hug his slim waist, long, strong legs and something else I don't want to spend too much time thinking about. I clench my jaw. None of that matters; I'm with Nicky. Even so, it's difficult not to make comparisons. Ash is taller than Nicky by a couple of inches and broader. Nicky has the body of a high-fashion model, while Ash looks like an athlete.

Ash motions me inside. I walk past him, and after my troubling reaction to him last night, I'm careful not to let any part of him touch any part of me. Once inside, I cross my arms and wait.

"I know things between us may have gotten off to a rocky start." He runs his hand through his hair as he comes to stand in front of me.

"That's the understatement of the century," I reply hotly. "And *for the record*, you might try asking the girl to marry you first. *Then* asking her mother."

"I tried getting in touch with you while you were still at Brown, remember? I asked you to meet me several times. You refused to see me. You stopped answering my texts. You changed your number."

"So you come to my court with a marriage contract? Just like that?" My tone is incredulous.

"Time was short. You had another offer on the table. I had to approach the Queen before she accepted Nick's contract."

"Why are you doing this?" The exact same question I had asked the Queen.

"My dragon wants you. And I'm forecasting a nice return on investment."

Return on investment? Is he for real? Is this simply a business deal to him?

He reaches out and takes my hand. My body swiftly reacts, an unwanted hum of desire vibrating through me. He pulls me toward the leather couch in the living room. "Let's get comfortable so we can talk."

It can't hurt to hear him out. I may learn something I can use to break the marriage contract.

He sits at one end of the couch while I go and sit all the way on the other end. I toss a couple of throw pillows into that space that yawns between us, keeping one to clutch against my stomach. I need a barrier between us. If he touches me, I may not be able to think clearly. He has an unsettling effect on me.

Pressing my lips together and raising my chin, I give him my best not-impressed face. "You were saying something about return on investment?"

"Well, first off, your mother is the Queen of Avalon, the Lady of the Lake. She's incredibly powerful."

If he's expecting me to be a chip off the old block, then the joke is on him. "I don't have her power, Ash. In fact, I don't have any power at all."

"I'll admit, that's unexpected, but I'm sure you'll get it eventually. You're just a late bloomer for some reason." He brushes an invisible speck of lint off his jeans, dismissing my lack of power. "She's also known to be shrewd when it comes to business, controlling one of the most profitable North American territories. You're in line to inherit all that someday. With our families aligned, we'd control more Earthside territory than anyone else."

The strongest rulers, like the Queen, had divvied up the territory of Earthside. Every financial transaction—legal, illegal, barter or trade—in an Earthside territory translates into energy on the preternatural plane, like supernatural bitcoin. More territory equals more power.

"Sounds like you're a big fan of the Queen. Maybe you should marry *her*," I suggest helpfully. Nicky and Ash couldn't be more different. Nicky isn't interested in the accumulation of power or Earthside territory. He's an artist and only cares about living life to the fullest. Unlike Ash, Nicky isn't a slave to tradition and doesn't want to fill the role of a typical royal son.

Ash laughs and throws an arm over the back of the couch. "She's a little older than me, and as you know, she's already married." Growing serious, he adds, "And, like I already told you, my dragon wants you. Since I turned twenty-five almost a year ago, he's been pushing me toward you. Filling my mind with images of you, urging me to follow you online, prompting me to text you. He won't leave me alone. He believes you're his fated mate. Apparently, you made quite an impression on him when you punched me in the face and split my lip open all those years ago."

Dragon shifters, as a species, are among the oldest magical beings and are known for their independence, cunning minds and immense power. But not a lot is understood about how their power works. Legend has it they don't simply wield magic, they are magic incarnate. They're a secretive race and live in small family clans. And they don't take well to outsiders.

"You talk about your dragon like he's a separate entity from you. Is it like having a split personality?"

"No, he's a part of me. It's more like we're flip sides of the same coin. We often know what each other is thinking and doing. Normally, we agree on things. But I'm not going to lie, his choice of you as his fated mate surprises me."

I push down my irritation at his last statement. "I guess being chosen as a fated mate is a big deal to you shifters. But is it real? Or is it bullshit? Be honest."

"He wants you and only you. He doesn't like me having sex with other females. So no, it's not bullshit."

"So your dragon believes I'm his mate. What about you?"

"I'm still getting used to the idea. Reconciling myself to it." He has the nerve to stretch, showing off the muscles of his arms and shoulders, seeming not to care how annoyed I'm becoming.

"You're *reconciling yourself?* So he wants me, but you don't? Is that it?" For some reason, that hurts.

"I didn't say that. You have a lot of upside, as we just discussed. You come from good stock." Ash's tone is contemplative, as if he's talking about a horse he might buy.

"I'm not a broodmare. In fact, if you read my info in the marriage contract, you'll know I'm the exact opposite. With my low fertility rating, it's not going to be easy to get me pregnant. So, if you're worried about continuing your family name or want lots of kids, I'm not the girl for you."

"I have two brothers and a sister. The Mountcastle name will be just fine." Ash leans forward, closing some of the distance between us. "And, Princess, I'm more than up for the challenge of getting you pregnant. I'll fuck you day and night if that's what it takes. I'll get you pregnant or die trying. There are worse ways to go." Ash schools his face into a thoughtful expression. "I want to ask you about something else I found unexpected in the contract." After a moment's hesitation, he asks, "Are you really a virgin?"

He has a right to ask the question. If anything is stated as fact in the contract, it can be questioned by either side. He doesn't know it yet, but he's just given me my out. "No, I'm not a virgin anymore. I was with Nicky." I look solemnly down at my hands as I bend the truth until it almost breaks.

Ash slides down the couch toward me, throwing the pillows between us on the floor. He puts his finger under my chin and lifts my face to his. "You're a terrible liar."

I quickly pull my head back before my body can respond to his touch. "I'm not lying. We did it."

"You can't even say the words. Did you fuck him or not?" Skepticism shines in his eyes.

"Yes." I nod and give him my afraid-so look.

"Say, yes, I fucked Nick."

"Yes, I fucked Nicky." I stare unblinking into Ash's face, ready to jump if he tries to touch me again and derail my performance.

"Tell me what you guys did in bed then. Tell me what you like." Ash sits back on the couch, his eyes studying my every movement.

"The normal stuff." I squirm a little under his gaze. "You know."

"No, I don't know. Why don't you tell me? In detail."

"Well . . ." It's difficult to accurately describe something you haven't done. I really hadn't expected this level of questioning.

"Go on." Ash prompts me, one sardonic eyebrow raised.

"Alright, I didn't sleep with him. But we did . . . other stuff."

"Well, now I don't know what to believe. One minute, you're saying you fucked him, and the next, you're saying you didn't. There's only one way to be sure. I want an inspection."

And then I knew I had fucked myself. "We never had sex. We were together in other ways."

"The poophole loophole." He smirks.

"No," I snap. "Not that."

"Yes, an inspection is definitely in order. Your mouth can lie, but your body can't." He slowly looks me up and down.

The inspection ceremony is an antiquated tradition that is rarely conducted anymore. Mostly because not many brides claim to be a virgin in their marriage contract and the results of the inspection are not always conclusive. It's an invasive physical exam, and he knows I won't want one.

"You know how it is with these marriage contracts—it's buyer beware. Got to make sure everything is as advertised. And Princess, *for the record*, I don't like being lied to."

"Go fuck yourself." This isn't about my virginity at all. He's trying to bully me.

"I'm perfectly within my rights to ask for one. And I'm going to have it. However, I think we can find a compromise."

"What kind of compromise?" I glare at him.

"I'll settle for an informal inspection. Just you and me."

"No way."

"Why not?"

"If I allow this informal inspection, what's to stop you from demanding a formal one later."

"You have my word."

"Your word means nothing to me." My tone is so icy I'm surprised I can't see my breath.

"Think about this, Princess. A formal inspection is you in a sterile white room, lying on a sterile white bed, in a sterile white medical gown. With how many people there?" He starts ticking them off his fingers. "Let's see. On your side, there'll be your doctor, the Queen and maybe her consort. Oh, he'd love that. Have you noticed the way his eyes follow you? I have."

I don't dignify that with a response.

"Then my side gets three representatives as well. In addition to me, of course. My doctor, my lawyer and maybe I'll invite Ben to watch."

"Are. You. Done?" My words are clipped.

"In front of all of us, Sofie will push up your medical gown and then spread your legs open so we can all see if you're a virgin. Or not."

I'm not listening to any more of this. I leap up from the couch and run to the door. As I turn the handle, he comes up right behind me and puts his hand on the door to keep it closed. "I'm having that inspection," he whispers in my ear. "It's your choice how it happens."

The heat of his upper body against my back makes me tremble. "I need to think about it."

"You have until midnight. If you're not back here by then, I'll take that to mean you want to go the formal route, and I'll start the paperwork."

CHAPTER NINE

B ACK IN MY APARTMENT, I lie on my bed and stare up at the ceiling as I relay the details of what happened with Ash to Kat and Sofie.

"But you *are* a virgin." Sofie, who's sitting on my bed, states the obvious. "I have your medical records to prove it. All of your exams are documented. He'll have to accept that as proof."

"No shit, Sherlock." I give Sofie a wide-eyed stare. "*I* know I'm a virgin. *You* know I'm a virgin. Even *he* knows I'm a fucking virgin."

"Anatomically, that's not . . ." Sofie starts to correct me.

I roll my eyes. "But I told Ash I wasn't a virgin. I told him I had sex with Nicky."

"Why would you do that?" Kat stops pacing around my room and turns to look at me.

"I thought it was my way out. It doesn't matter now. He played me, and I fell for it," I say.

"Hold on. I'm getting a call." Kat taps the side of her smart glasses and listens intently.

Kat loves her smart glasses and wears them instead of carrying a phone. Like a phone, she can use biomechanics to issue commands and open apps, but unlike a phone, the glasses use bone conduction technology, so she can listen to music or take a call without an ear piece.

Kat nods her head in agreement to whatever is being said on the call. "We're with her now. I'll fill you in later. I have to go." She taps her glasses to end the call and looks at Sophie and me. "That was Gia. She's in her weekly meeting with the Queen's press secretary and can't get away. She's sorry."

We all give a sympathetic shudder for Gia. The Queen's press secretary is an obnoxious old crow who loves to hear herself talk and never allows anyone, including Gia, to get a word in.

Kat comes to stand at the side of my bed and puts her arm around Sofie. "Are you going to go through with it, Nina? The informal inspection?"

"Of course she isn't!" Sofie answers for me, giving Kat an exasperated stare. "Let's try the medical records first. If

Ash asks for a formal inspection, the Queen will review the records and rule in our favor."

"Will she, Sofie?" I partially sit up, leaning back on my elbows. "Will she? She hasn't ruled in my favor once since this whole thing started. She's determined this marriage go forward. She's giving Ash whatever he wants. We're not going to get any help from the Queen."

"Speaking of help"—Kat pushes up her glasses—"I've hired a team of private investigators to do a little digging on Ash. See if we can find something to annul this marriage before it's consummated."

"Sounds good to me. But in the meantime, I'm going to go through with the informal inspection. I can't take a chance on there being a formal one."

"And speaking of what Ash wants, it's apparent he wants to get you naked." Sofie purses her lips, not liking the thought of me having to do something against my will.

"It's not the getting naked that bothers me. I don't mind him seeing what he'll never be able to have. It's that he outmaneuvered me. He caught me in a lie, and now he thinks he has the upper hand."

"I know it's cold comfort," Kat says, "but I'll submit an addendum to the marriage contract, stating that once an informal inspection has taken place, no further inspections will be permitted. We'll get Ash to sign it before you do anything."

"Fuck him. We'll see who feels like they've won after this inspection." I flop back on my bed.

As I stand outside the door to his apartment, I let my anger at Ash outsmarting me fill the sails of my confidence. To get ready for the inspection, I'd showered and put on a delicate pink lace bra and matching panties. Then I'd taken them off and put on a plain white bra and granny panties. Then I'd taken those off and put the first set back on. I'm wearing them for me, I told myself. Then I'd slipped on a black T-shirt dress that fell to my midthigh and slid my feet into a pair of flats.

It's 11:55 p.m. and after a deep breath to calm myself, I raise my hand to knock. The door opens, and I'm peering right into Ash's eyes. I drop my arm. *Awkward.*

"I wasn't sure you were going to come back." His voice is serious, his shit-eating grin nowhere to be seen. He tilts his head to the side, indicating I should enter.

I lift my chin and walk past him. The light of a single lamp now softens the decor of his apartment. "We need to set some ground rules. This is an inspection only. You can look, but you can't touch. I mean it. No touching at all. Also, did you sign the addendum stating you will never ask for a formal inspection?"

"I signed it digitally and just sent it back to Kat. Text her if you want."

I send Kat a text: *Addendum?*

She instantly replies: *Got it.*

"I agree to your ground rules. Now go into the bedroom." Ash directs authoritatively, as if he does this every day.

"Fine. Let's get this over with." Because the guest apartments are all basically the same, I know exactly where the bedroom is. I walk there with my head held high.

He follows me into the room and turns on the light. "Take off your clothes."

"You don't need to see my tits to determine if I'm a virgin," I spit out. "I'll take off my panties, but that's it."

"Take them off then."

I slide my hands under the sides of my T-shirt dress and hook my thumbs in my undies. Maintaining eye contact with Ash, I pull them down over my butt and shimmy them down my legs, letting them fall to the floor.

He extends his hand to me.

I disregard it as I step out of my underwear and kick off my shoes. "I said no touching, remember?"

Ash puts his hands up in the universal sign of surrender and then lowers them. "Do you want to change your mind?"

"Will you change yours about asking for the formal inspection? About going ahead with this marriage?"

He slowly shakes his head.

"Then I don't really have a choice, do I?"

"My poor Princess thinks she has no choices. Lie down on the bed."

I get onto the bed and position myself carefully so as not to give him a sneak peek. Don't want to let the cat out of the bag early, so to speak.

He grabs a pillow from the bed. "Lift up your butt."

When I hesitate, he lifts an eyebrow. "Do it, Princess."

I push my dress between my legs and lift up. He slides the pillow under me. Then I lower myself back down. With my butt on the pillow, my hips are tilted up.

Ash sits on the bed beside me. "Bend your legs and let your knees fall open," he commands quietly.

Slowly, I do as he asks.

"Lift up your dress." His eyes bore into mine.

For a nanosecond, my bravado completely deserts me.

"Do you want me to do it?" he asks.

"No, I'll do it." I lift my dress and watch as his eyes shift downward. Moving my hands between my legs, I defiantly spread my pussy open for his view, proving beyond a shadow of a doubt that I'm a virgin. On the spur of the moment, I decide to give my clit a few flicks to prove he hasn't embarrassed me.

Ash catches his breath and meets my eyes. "I could help you out with that."

"No thanks, I have it well in hand." I smirk. He's not the only one with a shit-eating grin.

His eyes lower to what my fingers are doing, and then he leans in. "What the fuck is that?"

My fingers still. Normally, these aren't words you want to hear in this situation, but I know what he's found.

He moves closer, still not touching me, to get a better look at the inside of my right thigh.

"It's a love bite. Nicky gave it to me. I told you we'd been together in other ways."

"Princess, there's no love involved in that bite. Are you really that naive?" He sits back and his eyes meet mine once again. "He marked you. Left a magic signature on you. Vampires use these signatures to enthrall their victims. Control their minds and bodies. Did you allow him to do this to you?" His eyes are tight, and his jaw is set as he frowns at me.

Sitting up, I pull my dress down. "Mind control? Give me a break. And it's none of your fucking business how it happened. I had a life before you showed up at my court with your marriage contract. My life didn't begin when you walked in the door." Ash thought he'd won with this inspection. He hadn't. I wanted him to find that love bite. See Nicky's mark on me. I'm the winner of this round.

Ash leans back on his hands. "When I asked for the inspection, were you hoping I'd be so cunt struck I wouldn't notice the mark?"

"No. Just the opposite. And I don't like that word. It has strong misogynistic overtones."

"What word? Cunt? It's a perfectly good word."

"I can say it. You can't. Don't say it in front of me again."

"Princess, you're pretty high and mighty for someone sitting there with no panties on. Get Sofie to heal that mark and get rid of the magic. If it's still on you the next time my face is between your legs, I won't be happy."

The next afternoon, I'm sitting on the examination table in Sofie's office, wearing a sterile white hospital gown. I can't help but be reminded of Ash's description of a formal inspection.

There's a light knock on the closed office door and Sofie calls out, "May I come in?"

"Yes, come on in." She never knocks before entering my apartment and has seen me naked lots of times, but when I come to her office for a medical exam or treatment, she respectfully steps out of the room while I undress.

She smiles at me as she enters, tablet in hand. "What's up? With your imminent marriage to Ash, did you want to talk about birth control? Even though your fertility is reduced, getting pregnant is still a consideration."

"I have no intention of fucking Ash, so birth control is the furthest thing from my mind."

Sofie lowers her tablet and looks at me expectantly. "Okay. So, what *is* on your mind?"

I fold my hands in my lap, then unfold them and intertwine my fingers. "I need you to do something for me. And I don't want you to judge me or try to change my mind."

"I think you'd better tell me what's going on." Sofie's tone is professional and her indigo eyes are unblinking.

"When I was Earthside, Nicky bit me. Ash saw the bite during the inspection last night and told me to get rid of it. He thinks Nicky bit me to enthrall me, which I don't believe for a second."

"Let me have a look." Sofie sets her tablet on her desk and dons a pair of thin latex gloves.

I lie back on the exam table and lift my hospital gown to show Sofie the two small puncture wounds on the inside of my right thigh.

"You know, Nina, Ash could be right about the mark. As a siren, I can use my song to create a psychic bond with someone and lure them to me. Vampires have similar abilities. With simple eye contact, a vampire can use hypnosis to dominate the will of another. They can also use their bite venom to establish and maintain long-term mind control. This normally only works on humans, but you don't have your power, making you vulnerable. Mind compulsion is very powerful and very dangerous."

When we were together, Nicky wanted me all to himself so we didn't spend much time with my friends. They don't know him very well and I feel the need to defend him. "Nicky would never do anything to intentionally hurt me.

And I'm not giving up his mark just because Ash told me to. I don't answer to him and never will."

"So what is it exactly that you want me to do?" Sofie asks.

"I want you to hide the mark so it's no longer visible on my skin. But I want you to leave the magic," I say in a strong and steady voice.

"Are you sure you know what you're doing? There are two types of males in the universe, Nina. Those who want to treasure you and those who want to target you. Are you sure you know which category Nicky falls into?" Sofie's stern tone signals her apprehension.

"The mark is all I have left of him, and I'm not giving it up for any reason."

"This goes against my better judgment but okay, we'll try it your way. I'll hide the puncture marks but leave the magic. I hope you know what you're doing." Sofie snaps her gloves more firmly into place.

CHAPTER TEN

E XACTLY SEVEN DAYS AFTER I signed the marriage contract, I'm standing outside the closed court doors. The consort stands silently beside me, and we're waiting for our cue to enter and for the wedding ceremony to begin. The Queen herself will perform the ceremony, binding Ash and I together until death parts us. *Unless I can find a way out.*

The past week has been surreal. The Queen sent her head seamstress to my apartment so I could be measured for a custom wedding gown. Whether the seamstress reported the specifications of my dress back to the Queen, I don't know, but she made the dress I wanted.

I haven't seen Ash since the inspection. Every day, I sent him a text asking him for more time. Every day, he replied asking to see me. It was a resounding no from both sides. Kat submitted petition after petition to the Queen, asking her to disallow Ash's contract, postpone the wedding, reconsider the consummation date, anything. They were all denied.

I have called and messaged Nicky every day, too, multiple times a day. I crave the sound of his voice.

I'm sorry. Please text me.

This wasn't my decision. Please call me back.

Call me so I can explain. Please.

There has been no reply. Why isn't he answering me? He sometimes disappears into his work, but he always comes back to me. It's been a week now and nothing. *Nothing!* I check my phone a hundred times a day to make sure it's over-air-charging correctly, that it isn't broken or dead.

I also emailed my profs to let them know I have a family emergency and will be out of school for the last month of my senior year. Two of them told me to keep up with my reading, and that even if I don't write the final, I'll still squeak by because my marks are so high. I'd lose my honors, but I'd pass. For a moment, a whisper of hope I might still graduate hovered in my mind. Then I heard from Professor Hardyman—the authoritative battle-ax who teaches two of my finance courses and thinks every word she utters is golden. She responded that missing her lectures was unacceptable and that if I don't write the finals in person, I'll fail both her classes. My whisper of hope slipped away like smoke out of a chimney.

Sure, I'll graduate eventually. I'll get the two missing credits online once my life settles down. But I won't get to walk across the stage to accept my degree. I curse the Queen. But most of all, I curse Ash for turning my life upside down.

When the double doors to court open, bringing me back to reality, the consort gives me a final glower before stiffly offering me his arm. "You can never just go along to get along, can you? You always have to be difficult."

Funny, his disapproval of my appearance makes me feel a little better. As he escorts me down the aisle, I feel as if I'm stuck in a nightmare. My only flicker of happiness comes from hearing the faint gasps and whispers of shock from those we pass on the way down the aisle.

I'm dressed in black from head to toe, looking much more like a widow than a bride. My gown has a high neck and a full satin skirt that skims the floor. The bodice and long sleeves are covered in crystal beaded lace. A simple black veil covers my face and is anchored in place by my heavy crown. The veil hangs to my waist in the front and trails two feet on the floor in the back. A pair of Christian Louboutin mesh ankle boots complete my wedding look. In addition to my all-black attire, I'm also wearing Nicky's mark on the inside of my thigh. Another "fuck you" to tradition and everyone who's interfering in my life.

Gripping the bouquet of blood-red roses tightly, I walk slowly toward Ash, giving him the evil eye from under my veil. I chose the tightly-closed crimson buds to symbolize my virgin flesh and blood—both of which I'm sacrificing for Avalon.

Ash is standing straight and tall at the end of the aisle, exuding quiet confidence in his classic black tux. There are a thousand guests here, and I know almost no one. These are the Queen's closest friends, enemies, business associates, and political connections. The turnout is small for a royal wedding of this order. Must have been the short notice.

When we make it to the front, the consort leaves me with Ash in front of the Queen, who stands on her dais. I stare right at her, begging her with my eyes to stop this. She can do it.

With a tiny, barely perceivable movement, she denies my silent plea.

Besides my dress, I had made only a couple of other requests for this farce of a wedding. The first of which was, there would be no bridal party. It would just be Ash and me.

Next, only the Queen's personal photographer would be allowed to take pictures and those pictures would be released to the public *after* the consummation date. There would be no candid photos permitted. Upon arriving on Avalon, guests had to sign an NDA stating they would not discuss the ceremony with anyone who was not present, and they had to hand over their phones to the Gorm. As they entered court and later the ballroom, guests would also be swept by hand-held metal detectors to ensure no devices slipped through.

During the ceremony, I say the words I'm supposed to say, when I'm supposed to say them, going through the motions.

When the Queen indicates, Ash slips a ring on my finger that I don't look at. And after she says, "You may kiss the bride," Ash lifts my veil and kisses me gently on the lips.

A flash of pleasure passes through me like a lightning bolt jolting me out of the haze I'd been walking around in all week. But I don't kiss him back.

We're bound . . . for now.

After the ceremony, Ash and I go outside and dutifully stand for a handful of professional photographs taken in the perfectly manicured gardens surrounding the castle. Then we head back inside to the ballroom to accept congratulations and well wishes from the Queen's guests.

Between shaking hands, Ash inclines his head to me and says, "You look beautiful. I didn't realize it was traditional for brides in your court to wear black to their binding."

"It's not." I force a smile for those watching.

He throws his head back and laughs. "A statement then. I like your fire, Princess. And I still think you're beautiful."

"You look nice, too. I guess." In reality, he looks spectacular. The tailored tux shows off his fit, muscular body; the black fabric highlighting his blond hair. Not that I'll tell him that.

"Sweet talk will get you everywhere with me, Princess." He shoots the sleeves of his white dress shirt.

Letting his sarcasm pass, I ask, "Are your parents here?"

"No, they didn't come. I have Ben here as my moral support."

We both look to where Ben is entertaining a crowd by speed chugging a beer.

"They aren't interested in getting to know your new wife?" I smooth a hand down the front of my gown.

"Oh, they're *very* interested in getting to know you better. You're all we talk about anymore. They couldn't bring my sister, and they didn't want to leave her behind."

"Why couldn't they bring her?"

"She's only three. She doesn't have any power. She's too vulnerable to bring to a foreign court."

Was this the reason the Queen had rarely brought me with her when she traveled? She had been away from court constantly when I was a child, traveling between the planes for various diplomatic missions and business deals. She'd almost never brought me with her. Ash's court had been one of the few exceptions. Was it because I had no power? I was weak? A liability?

"Wait, your sister is only three years old?" I grin at the thought of Ash having a sister so much younger than him. "What's her name?"

Ash gets a silly smile on his face. "Dahlia. My parents call her their surprise baby. She's the boss of all of us now." Changing gears, he asks, "What do you think of the ring? If you don't like it, we can choose something else together."

Holding out my left hand, I look at the ring for the first time. The massive pink, emerald-cut diamond solitaire sparkles up at me. The stone, which has to be twenty carats, is set in a platinum band covered by white diamonds. *I love it!* "Well, I mean, it's way too big. I can't be wearing this when I'm playing with the dogs or down at the stables."

"Should I take it back? Get something smaller?"

"No!" I answer hastily, looking back down at the gorgeous ring. "I'll keep it. I just won't be able to wear it all the time." I give a long-suffering sigh.

"The struggle is real," he deadpans.

I burst out laughing. I don't want to, but I do. And honestly, it feels good to let go of some of the tension. Playing along, I hold my wrist as if it's buckling under the weight of the ring and grimace up at Ash with an exaggerated groan.

"Princess Seraphina, what *are* you doing? Can you not act with even a modicum of propriety?" the consort asks, his upper lip curled in disdain.

Of course, that is the exact moment the Queen and her consort would come to chat. The consort never misses an opportunity to point out my flaws. I open my mouth to provide an explanation when the Queen gives me a silencing hand. "Never mind, we want to talk to you both about something important."

"Yes, a project if you will." The consort says, speaking on the Queen's behalf. "Ashton, with your experience running the real estate division of your father's territory, we'd like you to evaluate the Queen's real estate holdings. Determine the value of each property, make recommendations on what should be kept, what should be sold. Advise on how to make the portfolio stronger. And the princess will assist you."

Ash smiles proudly at the mention of the work he does for his father.

Great. Just great. I get to be Ash's assistant. I have an economics degree from an Earthside Ivy League university. Almost. And to top it off, this job is for *my Queen. My mother.* That should give me some kind of home-court advantage, shouldn't it? Any good feelings toward Ash evaporate.

"I'd be happy to." Ash bows graciously to the Queen and consort.

I stand there, silently fuming, trying to remember how to breathe. In and out. In and out.

Ash places his hand on my lower back. The warmth of his palm penetrates the fabric of my bodice and heats my skin. With dogged determination, I try not to notice another kind of heat blooming between my legs.

The consort speaks directly to Ash, snubbing me. "It's going to take some time. The Queen's holdings are extensive. I've set you both up in a private office where you can work together. Since you're not planning an immediate honeymoon, at least for the next month, I thought you could start right away."

I almost choke on my own spit at the mention of a honeymoon.

"I seem to have some time on my hands." Ash shifts his eyes to me momentarily before continuing, "We can start tomorrow."

"Now that that is settled, a toast." The Queen holds her champagne glass high, commanding the room. Everyone instantly stops what they're doing and focuses their attention on her. "To Seraphina and Ashton. May they enjoy a long prosperous union."

Don't bet on it.

CHAPTER ELEVEN

"**Y**OU AND ASH ARE Instagram official," Gia informs me before my eyes are even open the next morning.

After we'd spent the expected amount of time at the reception last night, Ash had escorted me from the ballroom. We'd been followed out by knowing looks and speculative glances. *Little did they know.* Ash and I had parted company outside my apartment without so much as a good night kiss. I'd attempted to shake hands with him—this was a business deal after all—but he'd simply looked at my outstretched hand and walked away with a disgusted grunt.

I rub my eyes, trying to wake up. "What? The professional photos were not supposed to be released until after the consummation date."

I hadn't slept well last night. I dreamt I was being chased again. But this time, I was running through a dark house looking for somewhere to hide, but there was no safe place. I still couldn't see my attacker, but I could sense his presence right behind me as I ran. I woke up in a cold sweat and couldn't fall back to sleep for a long time.

"It's not one of the photographer's pictures. It's a candid shot. Probably taken on a phone."

"How's that possible? I specifically said no phones. The Gorm checked everyone. Who posted it?"

"Ash. To all of his social media accounts. Instagram, Facebook, Twitter, even Snapchat." Gia looks down at her phone and taps the screen.

"You have him on Snapchat?" I ask, sitting up.

"You don't?" she asks, her tone indignant at the thought.

"Let me see," I groan, taking her phone. There it is. Big as life. A photo of Ash and me standing together in front of the Queen. He's slipping that massive ring on my finger. We make a deceptively striking couple. He's so tall and blond, and I look incredibly petite standing in front of him in my black gown. The caption reads, "And they lived happily ever after. "

Don't believe everything you see online, kids.

"Are you fucking kidding me? What's he trying to do?" I'm completely awake now.

Gia takes her phone back. "Seems like he's trying to force your hand. You want out of this marriage. And he wants to keep you in it. It'll be embarrassing for the Queen if this marriage ends up annulled now that everyone knows about it."

"I'm going to kill him." I swing my legs over the side of my bed and plant my feet on the floor, my blood pressure rising to dangerous levels.

"He's gotten a lot of Likes and Comments on the picture. Mostly congratulations, but there are several women who've posted crying emojis."

"If they want him, they can have him," I grumble, heading to the bathroom to get ready for my first day of work—as Ash's assistant. Fuck.

"I'm going to have to like and comment on these, too. Repost them." Gia says with a grimace. "I should actually post the original. It'll look odd if you don't say anything. It's out there now."

"Handle it however you think is best, Gia. I'm going to handle Ash." I slam my bathroom door.

An hour later, I stride into the new office the consort has arranged for Ash and me, wearing a short olive-green dress and a pair of neutral heels. I'm carrying an African violet planted in a small white pot for my desk. I'm not wearing the ring Ash gave me.

Ash is already there, sitting at the desk closest to the window. He's head down at work when I slam the door behind me and explode, "What the hell do you think you're doing?"

"Good morning to you, too." He casually tosses the pen he's holding onto his desk and leans back in his chair.

"Answer me," I demand, placing the violet on my desk and then going to stand in front of his desk, hands on my hips.

"I'm working. Nice of you to join me. The Queen's real estate portfolio is even larger than I thought."

I'm not interested in talking about real estate right now. "Why did you post that picture of us? With that caption? And I quote, '*They lived happily ever after.*' Ha!"

"Ben posted it. He runs my social accounts. But he did it with my permission."

"How'd he take the picture? The guards checked everyone for phones."

"They didn't check the groom." Ash's voice is calm and flat, like a deep lake of still water. "I brought my phone into the ceremony and then gave it to Ben. What's the matter, Princess? Am I spoiling your plans to try and annul our binding? And don't be mad at Ben for taking the picture. He only did it because I asked him to."

"Don't worry, I know who to be mad at." If looks could kill, Ash would be a crumpled pile of flesh. "This binding is a joke. And you know it."

Ash scrutinizes my left hand. "It's not a joke to me, and it's definitely not a joke to my dragon. Where's your ring?"

"In my room. I told you I wouldn't wear it all the time."

"I want you to wear it. I want to see it on you." His jaw twitches.

"What aren't you understanding, Ash?" I throw my hands up. "This isn't happening. I'm going to find a way to break this binding in the next three weeks."

"Why? So you can run back to Nick?"

I swear his eyes are fading in color from hazel to a soft gold. "Yes, that's right." *Do I even want Nicky back?* The fact that he's not talking to me is confusing and painful.

"I have to know." Ash leans forward in his chair, placing his elbows on his desk and loosely intertwining his fingers. "Why didn't you and Nick ever have sex?"

"Nicky wanted to wait until we were officially engaged. Until we had the Queen's approval."

"I think he was afraid of your mother."

"We're not *all* animals." I give Ash a pointed look. "He thought it was more romantic to wait."

"It's obvious to me that you don't know him at all, Princess." Ash shakes his head.

"I do know him. And as *you* already know, we were intimate in other ways. I screamed his name when he sank his fangs into me." *Suck on that, Ash. Suck on that.*

Ash stands up and flattens his palms on his desk, his eyes glowing. "Listen to me, Princess. On the consummation date, if not before, I'm going to strip you naked, spread your legs and fuck you until you're screaming *my* name. And then we *are* going to live happily ever fucking after."

CHAPTER TWELVE

T HE DAY DAWNS BRIGHT and sunny, perfect for a ride. After dressing in my riding pants, a chambray button-down and leather Dubarry boots, I pull my hair back in a low ponytail and head out.

Walking down to the stables, I think about the three ways Kat said we could potentially break Ash's contract and have the binding annulled.

One. If he had misrepresented his name. He was not who he said he was.

Two. If he had misrepresented his character. For example, if he was charged with a capital offense not disclosed in the contract, such as rape or murder, on any plane.

Three. If he was already married or bound to someone else, on any plane.

Kat's team of private investigators is looking into all three possibilities. Although I'm not hopeful he's misrepresented his name—that would be too easy to check—I'm crossing my fingers he has a skeleton or a long-lost wife in his closet.

My thoughts are rudely interrupted when I hear Ash's voice behind me. "Nice morning for a walk."

I turn and find him unapologetically checking out my ass. "Are you following me?"

"Don't you have a high opinion of yourself?" His eyes sweep over my body as he takes his time meeting my gaze.

I cross my arms over my chest to hide the fact his scrutiny has made my nipples hard. "Then what are you doing here?"

"Like I just said, it's a nice morning. I was out for a run. Where are you off to?"

Looking down at my riding pants and boots, I retort snidely, "To a ball."

"Is it hard for you to walk," he asks, coming up beside me, "with that stick up your ass?"

There's no right answer to that question, so I say nothing. *The bastard.*

When we arrive at the French-style stables, which are as luxurious as the castle they serve, we're greeted by Gus, the head groom. "He's all ready to go. Been waiting to see you, Miss Nina."

I'd grown up in the stables, and had asked Gus and the stable boys to call me by my first name. There's no point standing on ceremony when you're mucking out stalls together.

Nickering and soft snorting sounds come from the shadows inside the barn.

"Thank you, Gus." Half walking, half running, I skip across the cobblestones and enter the limestone structure. The stables boast arched ceilings, two hundred horse stalls constructed of gleaming hardwood and wrought iron, and a floor you could almost eat off of. The Queen's mount of choice is the Arabian, and she has over a hundred of them, but I'm into something a bit more exotic.

And then I see him, standing twenty hands high with a shimmering metallic coat. He's tethered and wearing his tack and saddle. "Hello, you beautiful beast. Did you miss me? Did you? I missed you so much." I gently rub his nose and cheek as I gaze into his sky-blue eyes. Then run my hands over his withers and down his side.

"You're not serious. Is that a . . . ?" Ash asks with wide eyes and mouth agape.

"A unicorn? Yes, he is. Close your mouth before you catch flies." I'm secretly pleased to have surprised *him* for once. When I'm around Ash, I want to shock him, outdo him or torment him in some way. *Maybe I have anger issues?*

With his beautiful form and the sheen of his coat, my boy resembles an Akhal-Teke, but he's all unicorn. He begins nosing around my pockets, looking for treats. "You little beggar!" I laugh. Being home does have some advantages.

"I've never seen one in person before. They're so rare. Where did you get him?" Ash's voice is hushed.

"The Queen called in a favor with Zeus, and this guy was my twelfth-birthday present." I look at my unicorn like a proud mother looks at her newborn baby.

"Twelfth birthday, huh? I bet I can guess his name." Ash leans against the stall and gives me his know-it-all look.

I cut my eyes to him. "Do you actively work at being annoying, or does it just come naturally?"

"What do I get if I guess right?"

"Nothing."

"Good gods, you're no fun." Ash heaves a sigh.

"Fine, what do you want?" I have no idea why his disappointment in me stings a little.

Ash immediately perks up. "That's the spirit, Princess. I want a night in your bed."

"No way."

"Come on. One night. I'm going to be there soon enough anyway. Aren't you curious?" Ash's eyes twinkle mischievously.

"Not even a little," I return flatly.

"Well, I mean if you're *scared*, you don't have to take the bet."

"I know what you're doing, and it's not going to work."

Ash starts making clucking noises.

My unicorn shuffles his hooves and whinnies softly.

"Knock it off. You're scaring him," I say.

"I don't think he's the one who's scared." Ash straightens up to his full height and looks down at me.

I rub my unicorn's nose reassuringly. "If it'll shut you up, I'll take your stupid bet."

Ash reaches out and traces the five-point black star shape in the hair at the base of my boy's horn. "His name's Star, isn't it?"

"Ha! No, it's North . . . star."

"What now?" Ash puts his finger behind his ear, pretending he can't hear me.

"You heard me just fine."

"Looks like I'll be spending a night in your bed unless of course you're not going to honor our bet. Does he fly?"

"He's not a Pegasus," I reply dismissively and roll my eyes.

"Apologies. My mistake." Ash touches Northstar on his shoulder and then strokes his long, strong neck. Northstar leans into Ash's hand, soaking up the attention. Traitor.

I look at Ash's large hands on Northstar and think about what it would feel like to have his hands on me. My boobs, my ass, my . . . My mind is ripped from its trip through the gutter by the faintest puff of spearmint. Ash's face is mere inches from mine.

I manage to duck out of the way just as he's about to kiss me. "What the? Who gave you the green light to come in for a kiss?"

"Your body language, Princess. Your flushed cheeks, dilated pupils, hard nipples. And so you know, as a shifter, I have an acute sense of smell, and female arousal has a very distinctive scent." He smirks.

Oh. My. Gods. "You're delusional. I *do not* want you." I turn my back on Ash so he can no longer see, or gods forbid smell, my treasonous body parts, and I untie Northstar.

"You *do* want me. And I sure as fuck want you."

I quickly lead Northstar out of the stables. Once outside, I expertly swing up on his back and stare down haughtily at Ash. "I guess we're both going to have to get used to not getting what we want."

Riding Northstar away from Ash, I'm disturbed by my body's reaction to him. I chalk it up to being away from Nicky.

From the moment Nicky appeared in my life and I looked into his dark brown eyes, I've been on an emotional roller-coaster. When we're together, I'm ecstatic, as if high on something. When we're apart, I can't think straight and am anxious and irritable.

The night he marked me, he had just arrived home after a week away exhibiting his work. He texted me to meet him at his house. Overwhelmed with happiness, I changed into his favorite dress and practically ran there.

When I arrived, he was in his studio, packing up a box of paints on his work table. Stunned by his beauty, I stopped in my tracks as his gaze met mine. He beckoned me to him with a wave of his hand and I went without hesitation. When I was standing in front of him, he tipped my chin up and said in a soft voice, "I want to give you something. A gift. Would you like that?"

I nodded my head like an obedient child.

"That's a good girl," he said, hovering his lips over mine, just out of reach. He lifted me up onto the tabletop, the cool wood on the backs of my legs giving me goosebumps. We spent several long seconds staring into the depths of each other's eyes before he kissed me and said, "Lie down."

I did as he asked, my body trembling.

He lifted the hem of my dress and spread my legs.

Thinking he was about to go down on me, I closed my eyes in anticipation. That's when I felt his incisors graze the tender skin on the inside of my right thigh. "Wait. Stop," I said, trying to push his head away.

He hesitated for a fraction of a second before he bit me, penetrating me with his fangs.

My back bowed up off the table and I screamed his name as the first hit of pleasure permeated my blood stream. All the muscles in my body remained paralyzed with rapture while his fangs were inside me.

When he'd taken his fill of my blood, he lifted his head and swiped his tongue over the bite mark. Then he helped me sit up and placed his index finger over my lips, keeping me quiet. "You'll wear my mark from now on, Bella. But there's more I want to tell you. We're going to be married. You're going to be my wife, leave Avalon and live at my court."

I smiled happily back at him as if in a dream. "Yes, Nicky."

CHAPTER THIRTEEN

T ROTTING BACK TOWARD THE castle after a good hard ride, Northstar and I crest a hill, and I quickly pull back on the reins. In the valley below, there have to be thirty guys, half in shorts and T-shirts and half in just shorts, playing rugby. Deciding to take another route back, I'm turning Northstar around when someone shouts, "Princess. Come down here." It can only be one person.

Heading down the slope toward the group of males, I spot Ash immediately. He's one of the guys wearing only shorts. He waves me over, and I set Northstar on a slow pace his way. My gaze ricochets around his body like a pinball: the heavy muscles of his broad chest and thighs, his ripped abs, his sculpted shoulders and upper arms covered in large tattoos. All of a sudden, I have an urge to mount Ash and ride him.

When I pull up next to Ash, he glances up at me and puts his hands on his hips. "Spying on us?"

"Spying? Hardly! I'm riding home. Minding my own business. How was I to know you'd be out here, half-naked, playing games with your friends and"—I take a closer look at the group—"half of the Queen's personal guard."

"You're not going to say anything about that, are you? I wouldn't want them to get in any trouble? We needed more players than the guys I brought with me."

What does he think I am? Some kind of tattletale? Everyone knows snitches get stitches. "Of course not." I look down my nose at him. With a quick flick of the reins, I signal Northstar that we're out of here.

"Do you like rugby? Want to stay and watch for a little while?"

I might have imagined it, but I think there is a tiny hint of apology in his voice. "No, thanks. I don't even know the rules."

"Why don't you come down off your high horse, literally, and I'll tell you how the game is played." Ash puffs out his chest in what I swear is a direct challenge.

Remaining seated on Northstar's back, I consider the challenge and enjoy this view of Ash. I'm normally looking up at him. "Interesting tattoos."

"They're traditional among my kind."

"What do they mean?"

"They represent my clan and different rites of passage. Maybe someday I'll tell you about them."

Well, excuse me for asking. I leave him standing there, waiting for a few heartbeats before smoothly dismounting.

"You're never going to be easy, are you?" He mumbles under his breath.

"What did you say?"

"Nothing." He drapes his arm loosely around my shoulders, and we watch the game. Although my first instinct is to shrug away from him, I don't. The embrace is casual, and I'm enticed to stay by how fantastic he smells. His hair and skin are slightly damp with sweat, and his scent reminds me of warm salted caramel mixed with freshly cut evergreen boughs. It makes my mouth water. It also causes me to go liquid a little farther south.

"We're playing shirts and skins, and my team has the ball now." Ash points to the others wearing only shorts. "The object of the game is to move the ball down the field and score."

"If the object of the game is to move the ball down the field, why is that guy throwing it backward?"

"You're not allowed to throw it forward, but you are allowed to run it or kick it down the field. Those are the forwards there. See Luke? He's the hooker. And Max is the flanker. Ben is playing the number eight position."

"You made those names up." I pull out of his embrace so I can get a better look at his face and determine whether he's telling the truth.

"Would I lie to you, Princess?"

"Yes."

He laughs softly. "No, I wouldn't and especially not about rugby. There's a saying. Rugby isn't a matter of life or death. It's much more important than that." He puts his arm back around me and pulls me close as he shouts, "Damn it, Ben!"

"What happened?"

"Ben was just short of a try. We needed those points. We're tied."

"If you're tied, then no one loses."

"You don't play to tie, Princess—you play to win." The resolute thrust of his jaw and hard glint in his eyes leaves no doubt he's telling the truth. "At least I do."

I'm in the bathroom getting ready for bed and thinking about Nicky. *Where is he? Why isn't he talking to me? Fighting for me?* Looking back at our time together, I did see a lot less of him after he marked me. And when he could fit me into his schedule, he was sometimes distant and preoccupied. Our relationship has always been equal parts exciting and bewildering. *Do we still have a relationship?*

I'm brushing my teeth when there's a knock on my bedroom door. Thinking it must be a member of the household staff, I yell, "Come in!" around my toothbrush. As I'm leaning over the sink, spitting and rinsing, I hear Ash's voice just inside my bedroom.

"Well, who do we have here?" he asks.

Low growls. Steel and Silver are introducing themselves. Good.

Stepping into my bedroom, I see my dogs facing Ash. Their bodies are held rigid, the hair on the backs of their necks standing up, ears pinned to their heads and teeth exposed.

"Whoa, now, boys. There's no need for any of that." Ash soothes them in a steady voice. "I know you're just protecting the Princess, but I'm not going to hurt her. And I know you're big and strong, but I'm bigger and stronger." Ash growls low in his throat.

They stand their ground, but simultaneously tilt their heads to the side as if to say "What the fuck?" In pack hierarchy, Ash is the Alpha dog. And they seem to recognize him as the more dangerous predator.

Ash slowly walks into the room towards the dogs and gives them each a scratch behind the ears. They roll over on their backs, and he kneels down between them and rubs their bellies, the whole time talking silly nonsense to them. "Who's a good puppy? You are. Who likes a belly rub? You do." Soon he's rolling around on the floor with them, playing a game where the dogs run up and bark at him, and he playfully tries to grab their paws.

"Steel. Silver. Come." I call my dogs back to me.

They promptly obey and sit at my feet. They look up at me with happy expressions on their faces, tongues hanging out.

"Steel and Silver," Ash repeats. "Hellhounds. Very impressive."

"Yes, they're Black Shucks. They were a gift from the Controller of the British Isles when I was born. They're supposed to be guard dogs." I give the boys a reprimanding look, and I swear I see sheepishness cross their faces.

"Don't be angry with them, Princess. We were only playing."

I give the boys each a little head scratch to let them know they're not in trouble. "What are you doing here, Ash? And how'd you get in?"

"We had a bet, remember? And your guards let me in. They're hoping to make my rugby team." He puts his hands in his pockets and rocks back on his heels.

"You have got to be kidding me."

"We have a very good team." The smile on his face quickly changes to an expression of sexual interest when he notices what I'm wearing. My pj's are a cropped white tank top and sleep shorts. The former gives him a nice view of my pink nipples and the latter, the curve of my butt.

"I'm joking about the guards. They go above and beyond where you're concerned. Even when I told them we're bound, married, they still called someone, who had to call someone else to check and make sure it was okay to let me in. They kept me waiting outside your door for almost an hour. What's up with that?"

I don't respond. Perhaps at some point, I'll tell Ash about what happened to me. And what happened to the guard.

"I should have told your guards that you'd summoned me. That you demanded I come to your bedroom immediately and consummate this marriage." He waggles his eyebrows.

"Like anyone would believe that," I say on a laugh. He's cute when he wants to be. I give him that. "Even though I find you mildly amusing, you're not staying. Truth be told, I barely know you."

"Come on. We've known each other *since* we were kids."

"Correction. We knew each other *when* we were kids. Prior to this past week, we haven't seen each other in, like, fifteen years."

"Hey, we had a bet, and you lost. Even Princesses know a bet's a bet, right?" His eyes wander over me. "Besides, after seeing you in this outfit, it would take all the Queen's horses and all the Queen's men to drag me out of here. Do you want to be the cause of that kind of disturbance?"

I didn't want him to be able to call my honor into question because I'd gone back on a bet. He'd hold it over my head and never let it go. I also didn't want the Queen to find out there had been any type of disturbance involving Ash and my bedroom. If she thought I was rebelling against this marriage, she'd probably move him in permanently.

I take too long to answer, and Ash must sense he has me on the ropes. "Or maybe you're afraid you won't be able to keep your hands off me?"

This is a very real concern for me. My body wants him, even if my brain doesn't. But now that he's thrown down the gauntlet, it galvanizes my resolve to resist him. It's like putting on a full suit of armor. I'm impervious to his charm.

"Okay, one night and *just sleeping*. I still have a few weeks before the consummation date."

His voice turns serious. "We'll just sleep. I promise."

I pull back the covers and climb between the fresh, cool sheets. Sitting propped up by a mountain of pillows, I wait for Ash to join me.

"Where do the boys sleep?" He eyes the dogs.

"With me, of course."

"Not tonight. Steel. Silver. Come." He pats the side of his thigh as he walks across my bedroom. "Sorry, boys, you're in the living room tonight."

"Why can't they stay in here with us?"

"My dragon won't be able to relax with two other predators nearby. He doesn't know them well enough yet. I won't get any sleep."

When the dogs are on the other side of my closed bedroom door, Ash starts shucking his clothes. His body is beautiful. All lightly tanned skin, chiseled muscles . . . and those tattoos. When he goes to push down his boxers, I hold up a hand. "No way, Jose. Those stay on."

"Are you sure?"

"A hundred and ten percent."

"Your loss." He shrugs his shoulders and then walks around to the other side of the bed. He tosses a bunch of the pillows on the floor and gets into bed with me. "Not my normal side, but I'm sure I'll get used to it."

"Speaking of sides of the bed. You better stay on yours. All night. My guards are right outside. One peep from me, and they'll break the doors down to get in here. And I won't care what kind of disturbance that creates." I turn the lights out and stare into the darkness, listening to Ash's quiet breathing, wanting to ask him about his tattoos.

"You don't have a thing to worry about." His voice is as soft as velvet and as rich as chocolate. "I'll be on my best behavior."

CHAPTER FOURTEEN

I WAKE UP TO Ash at my back in the big spoon position, his arm slung over my waist. I hate to admit it, but I slept soundly last night with him here. No nightmares. And waking up next to him is kind of nice, too. His breathing is deep and even, his body warm and inviting. So inviting, I snuggle deeper into his embrace. Sometime during the night, I lost my metaphorical suit of armor. Thankfully, my tank top and sleep shorts, as well as his boxers, are still in place.

"I know you're awake," he whispers. His hand begins drawing lazy circles over my stomach.

I give a sleepy yawn. "You said we'd only sleep if I let you stay the night. That you'd be on your best behavior."

"We did only sleep. And I was on my best behavior. This is a new day. All bets are off." His morning voice is a sexy rasp.

"I should have known better," I say without heat.

"If you want me to go, just tell me, and I'll go." Ash props himself up on an elbow and kisses my shoulder, his other hand continuing to lightly skim over my belly.

The problem is, I don't want him to go.

Keeping my eyes closed, I roll onto my back. Wrapping my arms around his neck, I lift my face to his. There's no harm in a little kissing, right? I mean, he is my husband. For the time being.

Ash moves partially over me, a warm hand on my hip, his face lowering to mine. His lips are soft, and there's no demand in the kiss, only coaxing. I open my mouth, responding to the gentle pressure. When his hand moves from my hip to hold the side of my face, and he deepens the kiss, the pleasure synapses in my brain start firing, and my critical thinking shuts down completely. Our tongues touch and move away in a delicate dance, causing sparks of delight to ignite all over my body. Ash sucks my bottom lip into his mouth, making my toes curl, before breaking the kiss.

He sits up to face me, pushes the covers down and places his hand on my right knee. "Did you get rid of that mark?"

"See for yourself."

He bends my knee, and I help him out by spreading my legs. Then he pushes my sleep shorts up out of the way so he can see the inside of my right thigh. Using the tip of his index finger, he traces the spot where Nicky's bite mark used to be. "My dragon is very happy that the bite is gone. He hated seeing someone else's mark on you." Ash gives me a heart-melting smile and settles on top of me, his hips resting in the cradle of my spread thighs, his mouth close to my ear. "Especially a fucking vampire's."

The mark is still there, of course, just under the surface of my skin. But with Nicky giving me the cold shoulder, I'm starting to think maybe I made a mistake asking Sofie not to remove his magic. *Did Nicky ever love me? Was it all a lie?*

I wrap my arms around Ash to keep him close. His weight feels so right on top of me. He kisses my neck and behind my ear as he presses the length of his erection to my core. He's built to scale. Slowly, he rocks back and forth until I'm consumed with desire. The only barrier between us is a couple of thin layers of material, and they're doing nothing to prevent him from hitting my clit just right.

I should tell him to stop touching me, and I should most definitely stop touching him, but I can't find the words or the resolve. Something in him is calling to me, and my body is answering. Is this what it's like to be a fated mate?

My bedroom door flies open, and Sofie strolls in, looking down at her tablet, the end of a stylus in her mouth. "Morning, morning," she says absently as she stretches her tablet to increase the size of the display.

"What the fuck?" Ash yells as he rolls off me. "Ever hear of knocking?" He pulls the sheet up to cover his chest like an outraged virgin.

Sofie wears an inscrutable expression. "Relax. I've seen it all before. I'm a doctor."

"You're not my doctor."

"No, I'm hers." She points her stylus at me. "So you'd better get used to having me around. Her health and well-being are my top priority. I take her temperature every morning so I can chart her cycle."

The temperature thing is a lie. Kind of. I have a microchip implanted in my shoulder that checks, records and transmits my vital signs to Sofie once every hour. The Queen insisted we both get the chips a year ago as a defensive measure after there'd been an assassination attempt on her life.

My increased heart rate must have tipped Sofie off as to what was going on in here, and she was trying to save me from Ash. And myself. After Ash fell asleep last night, I texted Sofie to let her know he was staying over. I'd also let her know I might need her cockblocking support if I had a moment of weakness. Ash's comment last night about me not being able to keep my hands off him hit a little too close to home.

Ash aggressively throws the covers back and gets out of bed. He stands there for a moment, glorious in his obviously tented boxers. Not bothering to try to hide his massive erection, he strides to the bathroom, scooping up his clothes on the way.

Sofie stares after him until the bathroom door closes. "Now that's what I call big-dick energy."

What can I say? It's true. I still raise my eyebrows at her.

"What? I'm just admiring a fine physical specimen of the dragon-shifter species."

"Never mind him," I say under my breath. "Thank you. That was close. I was wavering."

"*Wavering?* From what I saw, you had lowered the drawbridge and were welcoming him in to mount your castle. If I hadn't shown up when I did, the deal would be done."

"You're hilarious. Seriously, it all happened so fast. He must have used his power on me. Dragon magic is a mystery to everyone."

"It's not magic. It's hormones. If you want him, Nina, have him. I can't keep walking in on you guys. It'll get back to the Queen."

"That's just it. I'm not sure what I want." Falling back on the pillows, I question just how thankful I am that Sofie saved me.

Later that morning, Ash and I are at our desks in the office. After he'd dressed and left, I'd grabbed a shower and spent a little extra time with my handheld shower head, finishing what Ash had started. Now I'm feeling relaxed and refreshed in a blush A-line dress and wedge heels.

Sneaking a peek at Ash while pretending to fuss with the African violet on my desk, I observe he's not looking nearly as relaxed as I am. His full lips are caught in a scowl. Apparently, he hadn't spent any extra time in the shower. My phone buzzes; it's a text from Kat.

Kat: *The investigators are chasing down a lead on Ash.*

Me: *Details?*

Kat: *None yet. But it's something to do with his time at university. See what you can find out.*

Interesting. Although I spent the morning rolling around in bed with Ash, I can't lose focus on the end game. I'll do as Kat suggests and ask him a couple of questions, try to get him talking. Maybe instead of fighting him, I should take a different tack. Use the attraction between us to give him a false sense of security. When his guard is down, he may let something useful about his past slip. All's fair in love and war. And this is still war.

Standing up, I stretch my arms behind my back, which pushes my boobs forward. Then I walk around to the front of my desk and lean my butt against the edge, stretching my legs out in front of me. "So, tell me about yourself. Where'd you go to school?" Okay, that probably wasn't the smoothest segue.

"University of Melbourne." His hot gaze follows me over his laptop screen.

"Did you have a serious girlfriend there?"

"I had girlfriends. I wouldn't call any of them serious."

"What were their names?"

"What's with all the questions?"

"Just trying to find out more about you. It's one thing to read about you in a contract, it's another to get to know you in real life."

Ash walks around his desk and comes to stand in front of me. "Here's what I think. I think you're trying to pump me for information, hoping to find something that you and Kat can use to break the contract."

No one can accuse him of being gullible, that's for sure. "Not at all." I press a hand to my chest, right over my heart. As the words leave my mouth, I watch his eyes turn from their normal green-brown to coppery gold, and another question pops to mind. "What do you look like when you shift into your dragon?"

"Big." He takes another step forward and leans down to place his hands on my desk, on either side of me. We're nose to nose, and I can feel the heat coming off his big body.

"So, more of the same." I check out my manicure, feigning indifference to his proximity and fighting the urge to climb him like a tree.

"Yes, I'm a big, scary, fire-breathing dragon. You should remember that. Especially when it comes to trying to annul our marriage. We're bound together, and *don't you forget it*."

"Your eyes are changing color. Is that part of your shift? Can you shift whenever you want? Can you shift right now? Do you have to shift at the call of the moon?" I'm trying to annoy him with all my questions. And from the glow of his eyes to the way his lips are thinning, I think it's working.

"I'm not your hellhounds or your unicorn. I'm not a toy for you to play with, and I don't shift on anyone's command. Least of all yours, *Princess*."

My refreshed and relaxed vibe disappears. "When most people use my title, they do it with *respect.* *Y*ou might want to remember *that.*"

Then his lips are on mine, firm and demanding. When I open my mouth and kiss him back, his lips soften to a caress. Streaks of heat shoot south as he sweeps his tongue into my mouth and his hand gently cups my breast.

"Ash, I need you to sign—" Ben walks into our office, and I turn my head away, pressing my fingers to my lips.

Ben doesn't miss a beat. "Oh hey, Nina. I didn't realize you were in already."

"Ben. Out." Ash straightens and points to the door.

Our office door clicks shut, and I assume Ben is on the other side of it. I'm too busy trying to collect myself to turn around and check.

Ash exhales loudly. The moment is gone. "I'm going to New York to tour some of the Queen's properties. And you're coming with me."

"Am I?" I give him a "you're not the boss of me" look.

"You're my assistant, aren't you?" He smiles, knowing I hate that. "Plus, it'll give us a chance to spend some time alone together." He looks pointedly at the doorway Ben had just been standing in. "We'll leave the day after tomorrow."

It's a business trip, so there's no reason for me to refuse to go. And on the surface, it has to look as if I'm using the time until the consummation date to get to know him better. But a repeat performance of this morning will not be happening. "I'll go to New York with you. But just like on any other business trip, I won't be sleeping with the boss." Even if Nicky and I are no longer together, I can't forget that Ash is the enemy.

"Sofie, I'm dying." Our scientists had cured the viruses that caused the Rampages, and yet they couldn't unravel the mystery of period cramps. It didn't seem fair.

"Medically speaking, you're not, but I know you're in pain. Here, take these. They'll make you feel better." Sofie hands me two pills and a tall glass of water.

Sitting up in bed, I swallow the pills, put the glass of water on my side table and then curl back up under the covers. The arrival of my period at least partially explains my rolling around with Ash in bed the other morning. I get super turned on right before my period starts. Must be all the extra hormones floating around.

"Can you text Ash for me? Tell him I won't be in today." I didn't get my period on a regular basis, but when it came, it came with a vengeance. Nausea, fatigue, but worst of all were the cramps. They buckled my knees. I couldn't get out of bed for a day, sometimes two.

"Sure, no problem. I'll let him know. Try to go back to sleep for a while. You'll feel better when you wake up." Sofie gives my shoulder a sympathetic squeeze and leaves me to my misery.

I'm nodding off, slipping into the cloudy world of sleep, when I hear my bedroom door open. Assuming it's Sofie, I keep right on nodding off.

"What's this? Skipping out on work to sleep in?" Ash's voice brings me out of my sleepy haze.

I crack open one eye. "I need to replace my guards."

"Actually, Sofie let me in this time. You and I had a meeting this morning." Ash is dressed in gray dress pants and a black knit sweater that shows off the muscles of his arms and shoulders. He looks delicious.

I guess Sofie really is done with cockblocking duty. "I know. I'm sorry. I asked Sofie to text you. Didn't you get her message?"

"I got it. I came to make sure you weren't blowing me off for no reason. What's wrong? Why are you still in bed?"

"I'm just not feeling well." I close my eyes again, hoping he'll take the hint and go away. No such luck.

"What's the matter?" He peers down at me.

I don't want to discuss my period with him. Talk about an overshare. "Nothing. A headache." I throw my arm over my eyes in a move I know is too much drama for your mama.

"That time of the month? Aunt Flow visiting?"

"Do you have to be so much? All the time?" I take my arm from my face and prop myself up against my pillows. I guess I'm not going back to sleep anytime soon.

"Princess, you're so easy to rile up. Really, it's like shooting fish in a barrel with you."

"What are you doing here, Ash?" I'm tired, in pain and in no mood for sparring with him.

"I came to see if you were okay." His voice and his eyes both seem to hold a note of sincerity.

"I'm fine, really. You can go now." Truth be told, I feel like shit.

"You don't sound fine. Can I get you anything?"

Well, since he's here, and he's offering. "A cup of tea might be nice."

"One cup of tea coming up." He puts his hands in the pockets of his dress pants and strolls out of my bedroom.

I tilt my head to the side and bite my bottom lip, checking out his ass as he walks away. Gods save me. His body is a work of art.

I hear him rustling around in my kitchen. "You've got a hundred kinds of tea in here. Pick your poison, Princess," Ash calls out.

"Anything herbal. No caffeine. I want to go back to sleep." Hint, hint.

A few minutes later, Ash comes back into my bedroom carrying a large, steaming mug. "Careful, it's hot," he says before handing it to me.

I take the mug by the handle and then cradle it between my two hands. Blowing on it before taking a sip, I sigh in pleasure. "Apple and cinnamon. My favorite. How'd you know?"

"Cause you're made of sugar and spice and everything nice." He smiles as he recites the children's rhyme and sits down on the edge of my bed. "Can I get you anything else?"

"No, thank you. This is perfect. Sofie gave me a couple of painkillers just before you got here. I'm probably going to be asleep in two minutes." I swallow another sip of tea and then yawn broadly to prove my point.

Ash reaches over and lightly strokes up and down my arm. It's not the least bit sexual, but it's oddly intimate. When I was a girl, Gia used to do this to help me fall asleep. Ash's gesture reminds me of that. Of comfort and friendship. *Has Nicky ever done anything like this for me? Taken care of me when I wasn't feeling well? Shown me this level of tenderness? The answer is no.*

When I yawn again and have to fight to keep my eyes open, Ash lifts the mug from my hands and places it on the side table. I cuddle back under the covers and close my eyes.

"Go to sleep, Princess," Ash says as he kisses the top of my head.

CHAPTER FIFTEEN

T HE NEXT MORNING, ASH and I are standing in the office, ready to go Earthside. He eyes my two extra-large suitcases but says nothing. I shrug my shoulders and beam a smile at him.

With a flash of light, Ash releases enough energy to jump both of us to New York City. We arrive in the living room of a penthouse condo the Queen owns. It's a four-bed, four-bath with great views of Central Park.

"Have you ever been to New York before," I ask, after we drop our luggage in our respective bedrooms.

"This is my first time. I'm a virgin. You can break me in."

I disregard his obvious attempt at flirting. "If by that you mean showing you the sights, let's get started."

While we're waiting for the elevator to go down to the lobby, Ash's hand brushes mine. I pull my hand back but not before a current of excitement dances across my skin. "Gia arranged a private driver for us while we're here, on this business trip," I say, trying to remind both of us why we're here and break the climbing tension in the air.

Because Earth is the heaviest plane, it takes a lot of energy to teleport once here, so we'll travel using conventional means. Also, we can't be popping in and out of places. It upsets the humans.

In the lobby, the doorman lets us know our ride is out front. We leave the condo building and climb into the back of a black Audi SUV waiting at the curb. The driver, who introduces himself with a "Hi guys, I'm Sheldon," lays out our itinerary. When I notice the New York Public Library is a stop, I ask Sheldon to skip it. I've spent the last four years of my life in a library.

We start in Midtown, and after a quick stop at the Chrysler Building, we head to Grand Central Terminal. While driving, Sheldon points things out and tells us stories about each landmark we're about to visit. In the back seat of the SUV, Ash's large body and his warm, fresh scent fill the space. Even though we aren't touching, I feel surrounded by him and have to fight the urge to rub up against him like a cat.

In the Grand Central Terminal's main concourse, we admire the teal ceiling displaying its string of astrological signs, and I point out the small area that has not been restored. Ash listens attentively and smiles as I do my best tour guide impression. When we stroll hand in hand over to the famous clock and circular information booth, I list off some of the movies they've been featured in and announce we need to take a few selfies.

"Why do girls always want to take selfies?" Ash grumbles good naturedly.

"We like to capture the moment. Can you take it? You're taller. The angle's better."

Ash pulls out his phone and puts an arm around me, his hand resting on my hip. "Fine. If this is what I have to do to get my arms around you."

Leaning into him, I lay my head on his chest, right over his heart, as if it belongs there. *What the fuck am I doing?* Ash takes the picture and I quickly step out of his embrace before I do something else stupid. "Would you like to see my favorite place in all of New York?"

"I'd love to see your favorite place, Princess." Ash grins at me. "Show me yours, and I'll show you mine." His suggestive, low-pitched tone leaves no doubt about the location of his favorite spot.

Ignoring his banter, I slip back into tour guide mode. "The whispering gallery, located on the lower level, is made up of four archways connected in a square. When you whisper something into an arch, someone standing at the arch diagonal from yours can hear what you say despite the noise and distance."

"That's a pretty cool architectural achievement. Lead the way."

He's interested in what I have to say. Happiness unexpectedly fills me.

When we arrive at the whispering gallery, Ash walks to one arch, and I go to the one diagonal. I lean in and hear Ash say as clear as if he were right beside me, instead of thirty feet away. "You'll soon be mine, Princess."

To which I whisper back, "In your dreams." *Do I want to be with Ash?* Nicky always told me that if I didn't have him, I wouldn't have anybody. And I believed him . . . until now.

Next stop is the Brooklyn Bridge. "Let's get out and walk across," Ash says. We hop out of the SUV and start the trek. He takes my hand and I let him, liking the connection and feeling of belonging.

Could our arranged marriage actually work? If you think about it, aren't all marriages arranged on some level? No matter who you are, you want your parents and friends to approve of the person you're going to marry. Should I give this marriage a chance? We do have a lot in common.

First. We're both from royal families and have been raised to put our responsibilities before all else. *In addition to this fact, he's super gorgeous.*

Second. Even though he loves to annoy the fuck out of me, he claims I'm his fated mate. This is supposed to be something mystical and highly sought after by shifters, so I don't think he'd ever betray me. *Even though his mouth and the rest of him is made for sin.*

Third. We both know what we're getting. With the thoroughness of the marriage contract, there probably wouldn't be any nasty surprises. He knows going in it won't be easy to get me pregnant. And I knew that if anyone can do the job, he can. *He's already given me a taste of the great job he can do.*

Halfway across the bridge, Ash stops walking and takes his phone out. "Wouldn't want to miss the moment." He puts his arm around me and pulls me to his side. I slide an arm around him, too, and he snaps a selfie of us smiling like human tourists on vacation. The vibe between us is suddenly so easy, so natural.

When we finally climb back into the Audi at the end of our first day, I'm exhausted.

"I'm starving. What do you want to do for dinner?" Ash asks, still holding my hand, his thumb rubbing gently over my knuckles.

"Would you mind if we get some takeout and eat back at the penthouse? I'm beat."

Ash's expression turns pensive, and he lowers his voice so Sheldon can't overhear. "I'm sorry. I didn't even ask how you're feeling today. Are you okay?"

I'm touched by his concern about my period and give him a small smile. "Just tired. Really."

We settle on Thai for dinner, and Sheldon recommends a popular restaurant. Ash checks out the menu on his phone and calls in a large order, most of which is his, and asks Sheldon to make a second stop for beer.

Back at the penthouse, we spread our feast out on the coffee table. Ash pours himself a beer and opens a bottle of red wine from the Queen's collection and pours a glass for me.

Sitting close together on the couch, we eat directly out of the containers. When we lean over the coffee table to select what we want next, our knees and elbows gently bump, causing small pulses of arousal to burst through me. But neither one of us moves away. As I watch his long fingers deftly manipulate the chopsticks, I think about what it would be like to have those fingers on me. In me. I squeeze my thighs together to release some of the building pressure.

"Want a bite?" He's holding a morsel of lemongrass chicken out to me.

I close my lips over the bite on the chopsticks and then slowly suck it off.

He inhales sharply and looks at me with half-lidded eyes. "I think you're going to be the death of me, Princess."

I sit back and give a shaky laugh because I'm starting to think *I* might be the one in trouble here.

Waking up with a stiff neck from falling asleep with my head on the arm of the couch, I try to remember where I am. Oh yeah, the New York penthouse with Ash. I look down to the other end of the couch, and there he is. He's in a slouched, seated position, with his hands resting on his stomach and his long legs stretched out over the coffee table. He's really cute when he's asleep and not talking. *Really cute.* I have to stop myself from sliding down the couch and pressing my body up against his. Even if I were ready to concede defeat and bang his brains out, I'm on my period, so that's not happening. Especially for our first time.

Getting up, I roll my head back and forth to get the kinks out. I spot the empty Thai food containers and start quietly gathering them up so as not to wake him up.

He stirs anyway. "Hey, Princess. What're you doing?"

"Cleaning up."

"The Princess doing manual labor. Hold on, let me get my phone. This is a moment that should be captured for posterity."

"I liked you a lot more when you were unconscious."

He grins. "Here, let me help."

Once we dispose of the containers, Ash announces he's hungry again.

"It's one o'clock in the morning," I protest, looking forward to going to bed.

"Come on, Princess. Live a little. We're in the city that never sleeps."

"Should we call Sheldon for a ride?" I ask. Ever since the night I was almost raped going home from an off-campus party, walking around after dark makes me nervous.

"Nah, we can walk. I checked a map on my phone and we're not that far from the Theater District. We can go for a walk through Times Square, people watch, mingle with the humans. And then we'll find a diner and get a late dinner."

"More like an early breakfast," I grumble.

We set out, and once I get my second wind, I have to admit it's pretty fun. The lights are still bright, and there are lots of people milling around Times Square. Mostly tourists coming from late-night shows and hucksters trying to separate them from their cash.

At one point, two topless women wearing nothing but thongs and headbands decorated with large red, white and blue feathers come up on either side of Ash, parting us. If their nipples are any indication, they're freezing.

"Hey there, aren't you a tall drink of water," one of the women says to him. The other adds, "I know a souvenir you'll want to bring home. Take out your phone. Let's get a pic."

I watch as each woman lays a hand on one of Ash's arms and rubs her bare boobs up against his jacket-covered biceps. Clenching my jaw and grinding my teeth, I'm surprised by the strength of my possessiveness.

"Thank you, ladies, but I'm good," Ash says, giving them each some cash. They walk away with several backward giggling glances at him.

"Friends of yours?" I inquire tartly when he finally makes his way back to me. "You might want to suggest they wear coats."

"Whatever happened to free the nipple?" he asks innocently. "Careful, Princess, I might think you're jealous." Then he pulls out his phone and checks a map. "There's an open diner just a couple of blocks away. Let's get something to eat."

The crowds thin out as we leave Times Square and my apprehension about walking around at night is back. Even though my brain knows the chances of being attacked with Ash by my side are low, vulnerability still swirls in my gut. Once you're the victim of a violent crime, you never forget the feeling of being defenseless.

We walk toward the diner on quiet, dimly-lit streets when out of nowhere Ash gives me a hard push behind him. I stumble to the ground, barely breaking my fall with my hands.

"You don't want to do this," Ash says calmly, standing to his full height. He isn't talking to me. He's talking to the three guys who've come up behind us.

"Fuck yeah, we do, mister," one of the guys says slyly.

"Empty your pockets, motherfucker!" another shouts.

When Ash makes no move to comply, the three guys share a quick look before two of them rush Ash. Momentum carries the three of them out of the hazy glow of the street light and into the shadows.

I try to get to my feet. My only thought is getting to Ash.

"Stay down, you stupid cunt," the one who'd stayed behind shouts in my face and pushes me back to the ground.

"You've done it now. She doesn't like that word. It's misogynistic," Ash says in a grave tone from the darkness.

There are sounds of a fight. Fists hitting flesh. Bones breaking. The late-night air becomes heated and crackles with energy. The smell of smoke fills my nostrils as if there is a campfire close by. *Ash's dragon magic?*

My attacker gives me a slit-eyed glare, daring me to move. Then he pulls a gun out of the waistband of his jeans and runs toward the fight.

"Be careful, Ash! One of them has a gun," I yell, standing up. Terror seizes me as I think about what could be happening to Ash in the shadows. There's three of them and only one of him.

"All I wanted was your money. Now you're going to make me fucking kill you," the guy with the gun shouts.

More sounds of scuffling feet, fists connecting with body parts and groans of pain.

I can't just stand here while Ash is in danger. I have to help him. Despite my fear, I run deeper into the blackness.

"Stay there, Princess," Ash calls out.

I squint into the dark. It's eerily quiet. The fight must be over. "What's happening, Ash? Are you okay?"

"Everything's fine." The timbre of his voice is lower than normal and as I search the shadows, I see two yellow eyes piercing the night.

When he comes back into the light, he seems larger somehow. Taller, wider, just more. "Are you hurt?" He runs his hands over me, scanning me with glowing yellow eyes.

"No, I'm fine. Are you hurt?" I grab his arms. "Did you kill those guys?"

"No and no. Come on, let's get you out of here." With a flare of brilliance that lights up the night, Ash jumps us back to the penthouse. He must have decided it's worth the extra energy and the risk of being seen. Back inside, the adrenaline from the attack wears off, leaving me shivering inside my coat.

"I'm sorry," Ash says, pulling me into a tight hug. Even over his jacket I can feel the muscles of his chest and back bunching and flexing, his powerful physique rippling with restrained violence.

"It's not your fault, Ash. Are you sure *you're* okay?" I attempt to pull down the zipper of his jacket so I can get a closer look at him, but he puts his hand on mine, stopping me.

"I should have noticed them following us earlier. I let my guard down. It won't happen again." His eyes still have a golden hue, and with his bulked-up size, he's dwarfing me more than usual.

POWER HUNGRY

This side of Ash should probably scare me, but it doesn't. All I can think about is letting the heat of his body chase my chills away. I try to wrap my arms around his middle, but he stops me by putting his hands on my shoulders, keeping me at arm's length.

"You'd better keep your distance, Princess. I'm still pretty worked up. I don't trust myself with you right now."

"You won't hurt me," I whisper.

"No, I'd do something much worse."

"What's that?"

"Take away all your choices." He turns and walks down the hall to his bedroom and closes the door.

CHAPTER SIXTEEN

T HE NEXT MORNING, I'M yawning as I leave my bedroom. My sleep was tormented once again by a night terror of being chased and hunted by an unseen male. But my tired eyes snap to attention when I meet Ash in the hall. He's shirtless, and his jeans are unbuttoned. He looks like a walking sexvertisement. He also looks back to normal after last night's attempted mugging—his eyes are a brilliant greenish-brown, and he's returned to his petite dancer's figure of six foot five, two hundred and twenty pounds.

"Good morning, Princess."

We stand looking at each other for a moment, before he gathers me into his arms.

Tentatively, I run my hands up and down his broad back, feeling nothing but the play of his muscles. "Last night. Did you shift into your dragon?"

Keeping his arms around me, he pulls back enough to look me in the eye. "I let him come out to play with those fuckers.

But no, I didn't shift. I try not to when I'm Earthside. I'm a little too eye-catching."

Although humans fully embrace our charismatic, beautiful side, they don't like us flexing our muscles with over-the-top displays of magic. It reminds them of the immense power imbalance. If you use your power to frighten the humans and it draws media attention, you'll be yanked back to the preternatural plane to justify your actions. Our leaders don't want the humans to be scared and upset—it's bad for business and public relations.

If you can't justify your power display, you'll face the consequences—a trip to see the Council of Seven. The Council of Seven is made up of our most powerful rulers and includes the Queen and Ash's father. That's a trip you don't want to make. A dragon in Midtown Manhattan for a trio of would-be human muggers would probably be considered an over-the-top display.

"Thank you for protecting me," I say sincerely. "I don't think I said it last night."

"While I have you in a thankful mood, what do you think about moving up the consummation date? To say . . . today? I'm free right now as a matter of fact." Ash looks pleased with himself as he leans in to kiss my temple.

"Nice try. But I'm not *that* grateful. I think we'll leave the consummation date right where it is." I try for huffy, but the smile in my voice betrays me.

I move my hands to his shoulders and let my fingers skim over his tattoos. The intricate, abstract designs cover both of his shoulders, upper arms and a portion of his chest. The outline of each tattoo seems to be similar, but the center portions are entirely different. "Will you tell me about your tattoos?"

Ash's face tightens, his expression becoming guarded. "What do you want to know?"

"What do they mean?" I ask, raising my eyes to his.

He looks down at his tattoos with pride. "They represent being a dragon, my heritage, my clan, and things I've done."

"This one"—Ash raises his right shoulder—"stands for strength and bravery. And this one," he says, indicating his left shoulder, "represents my first kill."

"What did you do? Who did you kill?" Gods, I sound worse than Gia trying to get Ash to spill the tea.

"Sorry, Princess. That's all you get." He steps away, heading toward the bathroom.

Damn secretive shifter! At least he shared *some* information with me.

Ten minutes later, Ash joins me in the living room. "Sheldon's waiting for us downstairs. Are you ready to go?"

"Yeah, just one more thing," I say as we collect our coats, "let's keep the little mugging incident between us. No one needs to know."

Ash stops what he's doing and focuses all of his attention on me. "Princess, what's going on?"

I feel as if I'm teetering on the edge of a cliff. Despite my best intentions, I've grown closer to him over the last couple of days. The more time I spend with him, the more I like him. Maybe it's not him that I'm opposed to. Maybe it's the fact that he's the Queen's choice. Have I been too hasty in my fight to escape this marriage?

I give him a long considering look. Sure, he teases and challenges me, but he also listens to me and honestly seems to care about what I think and feel. Which is more than I can say about Nicky. He was never particularly interested in what I had to say or how I felt. And the fact that he's broken off all contact tells me everything I need to know. He doesn't love me. Are Ash and Sofie right about Nicky's mark? Did Nicky manipulate me?

It's time for me to let Nicky go and give Ash a chance.

Leap of faith time.

I decide to confide a few things about my past to him. "The Queen, the girls, the guard, everyone just tends to be a little overprotective of me, that's all."

"What aren't you telling me? Hey, I told you about my tattoos." He crosses his arms and waits.

"You told me a little bit about your tattoos, so you get a little bit back. There are some things that happened to me, in the past, that caused them to be concerned. I just don't want them to overreact to this."

My past no longer traumatizes me. I know the sexual violence I experienced wasn't my fault and doesn't reflect on me, but it's still difficult to get the words out. Was Ash going to be his regular teasing self? How was he going to react? I clear my throat. "When I was a little kid, one of the Gorm Guard touched me . . . inappropriately . . . several times. It caused a big uproar. Then during my first week at Brown, I was almost raped by another student. A stranger." My heart races, and my breath comes fast saying this out loud to Ash.

His brows knit together. Then he quickly pulls me into a bear hug and rests his chin on the top of my head. "I'm glad you told me. That you trusted me enough to tell me. What happened to the guard? To the guy at Brown? Who do I need to kill?"

"No one. It's all taken care of. The girls killed the guard. And Kat killed the guy at school."

"I'm starting to like your girls. They may be all right, after all."
Then he continues in a more serious tone, "But from now
on, it's my job to keep you safe and I'll be the one doing the
killing." He wraps his arms more tightly around me, and his
steady heartbeat punctuates the truth behind his words.

For the first time in my life, I feel protected and cherished.
We've entered into a new phase of our relationship. A
cease-fire.

After touring two of the Queen's commercial properties in
the Financial District, we stroll back toward Sheldon and the
waiting Audi. I'd been blown away listening to Ash talk to the
property managers at each location. He'd obviously done
his homework. Ash's sharp business mind and commanding
presence are total turn-ons. I could listen to him talk about
net operating income and full-service leases all day.

As we reach the Audi, Ash suggests that, since it's just around
the corner, we should check out the Charging Bull. He wants
to get a first-hand look at the iconic symbol of the Financial
District—the large, bronze sculpture of a bull rearing its
horns representing a "bull market."

Opening the passenger door of the SUV, he fills Sheldon in
on the plan. Then Ash pauses and says, "You know what,

Sheldon? Take the rest of the day off. We'll take the subway back."

"Are you sure?" Sheldon and I ask at the same time.

"Yes, riding the subway is part of the full New York experience." He grins back at us.

"How would you know?" I ask.

"What do you think I was doing all alone in my room last night? Research." And then he adds for good measure, "I can't spend all my time jerking off."

Sheldon laughs merrily, his brown eyes smiling. "Okay, you guys, have fun. Call me if you need anything. You've got my number."

We head out and I almost miss how Ash subtly maneuvers me so he's on the street side of the sidewalk. The people on the street in the Financial District are a mix of casually dressed, slow-walking tourist types and sharply attired, fast-walking business types. Ash and I are a combo of the two—slow walking, but sharply attired. We're in no rush. This area of New York is beautiful with its glossy skyscrapers and cobblestone streets set against striking waterfront views.

At the Charging Bull, Ash stands for a couple of pictures. I tell him I *have* to take them because Taurus is his sign. Then we walk hand-in-hand down to the Staten Island Ferry.

After the attack last night, Ash seems a little more protective today and tells the dealers who aggressively try to sell us tickets to sightseeing boat tours to "fuck off."

We don't have a long wait at the terminal, and soon we're standing outside at the rail of the ferry, breathing in the cool, moist air. Ash stands behind me, bracketing me between his arms with his hands on the railing. Lulled by the gentle rocking of the ferry and wanting to be closer to him, I lean back into his chest.

"Is that it?" Ash doesn't seem particularly impressed with the Statue of Liberty. We're snapping a selfie in front of it anyway when he comments, "I thought it would be bigger."

"That's what she said," I reply slyly. The selfie captures us laughing our asses off into the camera.

After the round trip to and from Staten Island, we're back in Manhattan and descending the steps of a nearby subway station. Ash buys a pass at the ticket machine, which he swipes for both of us at the turnstile. Then I follow him to the platform. I have no idea which train we're supposed to get on. I've never been on the subway before. Normally, I ride in the back of a limo. Sorry, not sorry.

"How do you know where we're supposed to go?" I ask, my voice a little strained.

"I read the maps when we came in. Are you nervous?"

"No, of course not." Yes, for some reason, I'm very nervous. Maybe it's leftover anxiety from the attempted mugging or my nightmare last night. Or from telling Ash about my past this morning. I'm not sure. The panicky sensation seems to be welling up from somewhere deep inside of me, but I can't put my finger on what the problem is. I unzip my jacket, feeling hot and bothered. And not in a good way. My heart starts beating faster, and I'm finding it difficult to breathe. I try to take a deep breath to calm down, but I can't.

"Princess?" Ash mouths, looking down at me. I can barely hear him.

My field of vision narrows, and the world turns into a kaleidoscope of yellow and green.

"Nina?" I think I hear as I pass out.

I never get the full New York experience.

CHAPTER SEVENTEEN

WHISPERING VOICES PULL ME out of the blackness. I open my eyes to find I'm back in my room in the castle and the girls are surrounding me. "What happened? Where's Ash?"

Kat stands over me with her hands on her hips. "He was here. Then he left with the Queen. She wanted to speak with him . . . privately."

"Something's going on there." Gia blows a strand of red hair out of her eyes as she sits on the edge of my bed.

"What do you mean?" I ask.

Gia shrugs her shoulders. "I felt *undercurrents*."

I frown at Gia and then shift my eyes to Kat. "The Queen was here?" This is unheard of. The Queen doesn't come to you. You go to the Queen.

But it's Sofie who answers my question as she makes a note on her tablet. "She was the first one to sense something was wrong with you. Even before I could pick up the changes in the data from your microchip. She was waiting here for you when Ash brought you back. What happened down there?"

"We were underground, waiting for a subway. I felt dizzy and lightheaded. I couldn't breathe. Then I passed out."

"What do you think, Sofie? Panic attack?" Kat wants quick answers, like always.

"I'll do the diagnosing here, thank you, Kat." Sofie looks from me to her tablet, contemplating. Then she starts shooting off rapid-fire questions. "Did you and Ash have sexual intercourse?"

"No."

"I noticed an increase in your heart rate at one point last night. Did you have an orgasm with Ash or alone?"

"No."

"Did you have sexual contact of any kind?"

"We hugged. We held hands. That's it."

Both Kat and Gia whip their heads around to regard me. I'm guessing they're surprised we had even that much contact. Sofie obviously hadn't told them she'd found Ash and me in bed together the other morning.

Sofie, ever the professional, gives nothing away and moves on. "Did anything out of the ordinary happen in New York?"

I hesitate.

"What happened? Spill." Gia's eyes light up.

"If I tell you, you have to promise it stays in this room. I don't want it to get back to the Queen." I sit up in bed and give each of them an "I mean it" stare.

"Of course, ever heard of doctor-patient privilege?" Sofie sounds offended.

"And lawyer-client privilege." Kat's tone is equally miffed.

We all look at Gia. As my social media manager and publicist, blabbing stuff is her bread and butter.

Gia heaves a dramatic sigh. "Really, ladies? Really? Is this how it is now? Geez, cross my heart and hope to die. Stick a needle in my eye. I won't say anything."

I take a deep breath, needing to downplay this as much as possible. "Okay, we were attacked by some humans last night. They tried to mug us. Ash partially shifted, and then he beat the shit out of them. It was over in a matter of minutes. It really wasn't a big deal."

"Hmm, so you experienced, at least on some level, violence and shifter magic." Sofie looks up from her tablet.

"My exposure to the violence and magic was minimal. I hardly even saw anything. It was dark."

Kat pushes up her glasses. "What do you think, Sofie?"

"How do you feel now?" Sofie is still in the information-gathering phase.

"I feel fine. Totally normal." I raise my hands for emphasis.

Sofie lowers her tablet to her side. "I don't think it was a panic attack. I think it was a power flicker. Being threatened and exposed to Ash's magic may have triggered something in you. We'll keep you under observation for the next twenty-four hours."

I secretly hope Sofie is right and this is my power coming in, but I don't feel any different. It's not as if I'm shooting lightning bolts from my fingertips or anything. Besides, this has happened before, and my power never materialized. There were power flickers the first time I'd seen the Queen kill someone, as well as when I'd got my first period and had my first wet dream.

"I don't want the Queen to find out about the mugging," I reiterate.

"Yes, we all know where that will lead," Gia says. "You'll be put on a very short leash. She'll lock you up and throw away the key."

We all turn when my bedroom door swings open and Ash walks in, his hands in his pockets.

"Doesn't anybody knock around here?" I look directly at him.

"No, apparently not." He looks directly at Sofie.

"Don't mind us. We were just leaving," Sofie says, and the girls file out of my room.

When we're alone, I ask the million-dollar question. "What did you and the Queen talk about?"

"We talked about New York." He lowers his eyes to the floor.

"Did you tell her about what happened last night? The mugging?" I bite my lower lip, fearing I already know the answer.

He meets my gaze. "Yes."

My heart drops into my stomach. "Why? You promised you wouldn't."

"Actually, I didn't promise."

"That's just semantics, Ash," I shoot back. "You knew I didn't want her to find out."

"Nina, something happened to you in that subway station. You passed out and were having a seizure. When it comes to your health, I won't withhold information from your doctor. Or your mother."

So, Sofie already knew what had happened before we played twenty questions. *Everyone needs to stop fucking managing me.*

"I can't believe you, Ash." My voice drips with resentment. First I'm abandoned by Nicky and now I'm betrayed by Ash. My deep-seated insecurities rush up to the surface. *I'm not worthy of love or loyalty.* "The mugging and me passing out are probably not even related. Yet, you went running right to the Queen. Probably couldn't wait to report back to her. You two seem to have an awfully cozy relationship. I see where your loyalty lies now." I could have forgiven almost anything else, but going behind my back to the Queen is a deal breaker. I'm her sole heir and for that reason she's obsessed with my safety.

Ash's betrayal causes a tightening in my chest that hurts like hell. I thought we'd grown closer in New York, reached a new level of trust, called a cease-fire. Well, the cease-fire is officially over.

"It's not like that. She wanted to know what happened to you. That's all." Ash runs his hand through his hair.

Rubbing the sore spot in my chest, I stare icily at Ash. "Do you have any idea what you've done? She'll use this information to keep me under her thumb. As an excuse to continue to control my life and keep me on this island. You fucked up by telling her, Ash. You fucked up *royally*. Get out."

CHAPTER EIGHTEEN

I SPEND THE NEXT day in my apartment under Sofie's watchful eye and use the time to regroup and refocus where Ash is concerned. I give my guards strict instructions not to allow him to enter my apartment under any circumstances. He sends me a few texts, asking how I'm feeling. When I don't answer his third text, he stops trying to get in touch with me. I have to put some physical and mental distance between us.

Nightmares continue to plague my sleep, and they're getting worse. I'm running through a dark forest, tripping and falling over the underbrush, branches slashing at my face and arms. The shadowy male hangs back a bit, tracking me, stalking me. Just when I think I've gotten away, he pops up in front of me, forcing me to run in a different direction. He's corralling me, penning me in. It doesn't take a rocket scientist to figure out my subconscious is warning me about Ash and our arranged marriage. *What else could it be?*

Ash has shown me where his loyalty lies, and it's not with me. He's in league with the Queen. It's the only explanation.

She gave him whatever he wanted during the contract negotiations, and now he's sharing information with her that I expressly asked him not to.

My metaphorical suit of armor is back on where he's concerned. And this time, it's not coming off.

While scrolling through my social this morning before work, I saw something that jolted me upright in bed. Nicky commented with several heart emojis on a photo of me that Gia posted to Instagram. What kind of game is he playing? Ignoring all my attempts to talk, and then commenting on my photo. *Total dick move.*

Now, I'm back in the office, sitting behind my desk. It's almost lunchtime, and Ash and I haven't spoken a word to each other all morning. Both of us are using our laptop monitors as shields, reviewing spreadsheets and pretending the other isn't there.

Not quite sure how to break the stony silence, I skim my hands down over my raspberry capris and look across the office at him. He's in jeans, a black T-shirt and a ball cap with the New Zealand All Blacks logo on it.

"So, I was wondering something. How'd you know?" I narrow my eyes at him and put into words a thought that has been circling my mind since I found out he betrayed me.

"You're talking to me now, are you? How lucky for me." Ash doesn't look away from his monitor. "Know what?"

"How'd you know that Nicky had sent a marriage contract to the Queen? How could you possibly have known?"

"The Lady of the Lake's daughter getting engaged? That kind of news travels fast. You know how it is with royal gossip." He taps away at his keyboard, still not looking at me.

Something isn't right. "But she rejected the contract. She sent it back. Why would she have told anyone? It doesn't make sense."

He finally looks up from what he's doing. "Maybe she wasn't the source of the leak. There were doctors, lawyers, accountants and clerks from both families involved. It could have been leaked by anyone."

My bullshit meter is going off. "Well, it never appeared on social media anywhere or in any of the online tabloids. That I know for sure. Gia would have told me."

"Our parents are long-time friends and business associates. She must have told my folks and that's how I heard. Yes, that's probably it." Ash checks his watch, and his face changes to an "oh, look at the time" expression. "Listen, I have to go. I'm having lunch with Thane. I want to change my clothes before we meet."

"Thane?" I ask.

"The consort." Ash shakes his head at me. "I'm giving him a status report on our work so far. I'll see you later."

"Yeah, sure. Later." He can't even answer the simplest question and is on a first-name basis with the consort, the Queen's right-hand man and someone who's never been my biggest fan.

A few hours later, I push back from my desk and rub the back of my neck. Ash hasn't returned to the office from his lunch with the consort.

I'm thinking of packing it in for the day and taking off a bit early when Gia bursts into my office. "Nina, you'd better come."

"What's going on?" I can tell by the stricken look on her face and the brittle tone of her voice this isn't a joke.

"It's Silver and Steel," Gia says, wringing her hands.

"What? My boys? What's wrong with them?" I stand and quickly follow Gia out of my office.

"They're sick. I went to your apartment looking for you. I wanted to talk about your social content calendar for next month, and I found them. They were just lying there. They didn't move at all when I walked in. Which is not like them. Sofie is with them now."

We both pick up the pace, hustling through the halls of the castle.

When I was away at Brown, the girls had split their time between Avalon and Earthside. Whoever was on Avalon would spend time with the dogs, which is one of the reasons my apartment has an open-door policy where the girls were concerned. They love the boys as much as I do.

Barreling through the doors of my apartment, I find Sofie kneeling down with a small portable ultrasound device, examining Steel. The device is capturing real-time images of Steel's heart and is much more accurate than the old-style stethoscope. "Sofie, what is it? What's going on with them?"

Sofie stands up. "I'm not a vet, but I think they've been poisoned. I've sent word to the stables that we need Dr. Morrison. He's on his way up."

Silver and Steel are both lying on their sides, their breathing weak and shallow. Their swollen, purplish tongues hang out the sides of their mouths and their cloudy eyes don't even follow me when I get down on my knees beside them.

"How could this happen?" I blink back my tears. "What could they have gotten into to make them so sick?"

"Maybe *they* didn't get into anything. Maybe it wasn't an accident," Gia says.

"Don't be ridiculous. Who would want to hurt my dogs?" I look up at Gia and Sofie from my position on the floor.

"Someone who wants to hurt you," Gia replies.

Pangs of fear and adrenaline shoot through me at the thought of someone attempting to kill my dogs to send me a message.

At that moment, a guard escorts Dr. Morrison through the wide-open doors of my apartment. "If you don't mind, Princess Seraphina, I'd like to take a look at my patients."

"How are the boys? I just heard." Ash takes my elbow and bends to kiss me on the cheek. He's late to the party. Literally. He was supposed to meet me thirty minutes ago, before the formal introductions.

We're attending a black-tie gala being hosted by the Queen for the visiting Controller of Spain, Thiago Casado, a jaguar shifter. Unlike most big-cat shifters, jaguars kill by piercing their prey's skull with one hard bite instead of grabbing their prey by the throat and suffocating it. Thiago is legendary for his powerful jaws, impressive teeth and being a stone-cold killer. You wouldn't know it from his appearance—he's a good-looking guy with black hair and piercing emerald-green eyes. He introduced me to the beautiful blond dangling off his arm as Ana Morata. And if I'm any judge of magic, she's a witch.

"Tell me what happened." Ash is all bristling alpha male in a black tux.

"Dr. Morrison and Sofie think Steel and Silver were poisoned. That they must have gotten into something in the castle or maybe on the grounds. Dr. Morrison took them down to the stables and gave them something to empty their stomachs. He's texting me hourly updates. He says he'll stay with them all night, and I can see them tomorrow."

"I'm so sorry this happened. Are you all right?" He glides his fingers gently up and down the back of my arm. A shudder passes through me, and I'm not sure whether it's my body's reaction to Ash or the stress of what happened to my dogs.

"I'm worried about them. But Dr. Morrison says it's not easy to kill a hellhound."

"I'm sure Dr. Morrison is right and they're going to be fine." He pulls me into a hug.

A small part of me wants to rest my head on his chest and absorb the comfort he's offering. But I don't allow myself the luxury. Getting close to Ash during our New York trip had been a huge step in the wrong direction. I wouldn't be making that mistake again. I pull out of his embrace. "Gia has an interesting theory."

"Oh yeah, what's that?" he asks, keeping a light grip on my upper arm, which I gently extract by pretending to adjust my gown.

"She wonders if someone poisoned them on purpose. To hurt me. That perhaps it wasn't an accident at all." I watch his face very closely for a reaction. He gives nothing away.

"Who would do that? Who could do that?" He tilts his head to the side and strokes his chin thoughtfully. "We're on an island protected by your mother's power. Surrounded by the Gorm Guard."

"Who indeed?" I ask carefully, trying to read his eyes for a sign. A sign of what, I'm not sure. But he's looking over the top of my head and doesn't meet my eyes. "It would have to be someone already on Avalon."

"Do you think it's one of these jaguar shifters? They don't mind killing things." Ash scans the crowd.

"Poison is not exactly their modus operandi. They're hunters."

"Steel and Silver probably ate something they shouldn't have. Dogs do that all the time. The important thing is they're going to be okay." Ash tugs lightly on his bow tie. "Where are all the servers? I need a drink. Want something?"

"No, thank you."

When he finally makes eye contact with me, he takes the conversation in a whole new direction. "I noticed Nick commented with heart emojis on your Instagram photo."

"Yes, I saw that, too. What about it?" I'm totally pissed at Nicky.

"Are you still talking to him?"

I haven't spoken to Nicky since I got back to Avalon. But Ash doesn't need to know that, so I say nothing and give him a Mona Lisa smile.

"If you're still in touch with him, I want you to stop." Ash's tone is unyielding.

"I'll do as I please. I don't take orders from you." I peer up at him, a challenging glint in my eye.

"Whatever was between you two is over. Do you understand me?"

"If I didn't know better, Ash, I might think this arranged marriage means more to you than aligning our family's power or a biological directive to satisfy your dragon."

"Thank the gods you know better, then." His voice is hard, his expression turning frosty.

I don't know what I was hoping he'd say, but that isn't it. And for some reason, his ice-cold attitude hurts. *Why am I letting him get to me?*

I turn on my heel to leave and take several steps when the heat of Ash's hand on my back stops me. "I'm sorry. Please don't go. You've had a really shitty day, and I'm being a jealous ass."

"Yes, you're an ass. We've finally found something we agree on." But I stay. Mostly because it's an event hosted by the Queen and I would be conspicuous by my absence.

Ash doesn't leave my side for the rest of the night. He whispers silly made-up stories to me about the guests at the gala and does his best to take my mind off my dogs for the rest of the evening. But as hard as he tries to cheer me up, my intuition tells me Steel and Silver's poisoning was no accident. And there's more to Ash than meets the eye.

CHAPTER NINETEEN

I WAKE UP EARLY the next morning and, after dressing in my riding clothes, head down to the stables to check on Silver and Steel. The source of their poisoning is still a mystery. But if they're doing well and resting comfortably, I plan to take Northstar out for a long ride. Riding is my therapy, and Northstar is my therapist. He knows all of my secrets, and unlike the Queen, he never judges me.

When I arrive at the normally quiet and orderly stables, I'm met with chaos. Gus is hollering out commands, and grooms run back and forth across the cobblestones. I stop one of the grooms. "What the hell is going on, Nathaniel?"

His eyes widen when he sees it's me.

"Nathaniel, get going. This is no time for standing around," Gus shouts from inside the large limestone structure of the stables.

The groom takes off at a run, and I hurry inside to find Gus.

"You don't want to come in here, Miss Nina," Gus says from the shadows. "Best you wait outside."

"What's going on here, Gus?" I take a look around, and although I don't see anything out of place—the dark wood stalls and stone floor are as polished and scrubbed as always—the horses are snorting and blowing. Something has upset them.

"I've sent one of the lads up to the castle to get Ash. He'll be here in a minute. Just stay outside till he gets here."

"Why would you call for Ash? Has something happened to Steel or Silver?" If one of my dogs died . . . No, I can't even go there. Why won't someone just tell me what's going on?

"Princess, let me talk to you outside for a minute," Ash says quietly, coming up behind me.

I take a few steps further into the stables when Ash takes me by my right upper arm, stopping me. "Let me talk to you for a minute, please."

I jerk my arm out of his grasp. "Start talking." I cross my arms protectively over my chest and look defiantly into his eyes, hoping for the best but preparing for the worst.

He runs a hand through his hair before saying in a low voice, "I'm very sorry to have to tell you this, but Northstar is missing."

I stand stock still, trying to process what he's saying. This is the last thing I expected to hear. I can't speak. I can't breathe.

Ash's eyes are tight, his eyebrows furrowed. "Gus went to his stall this morning to get him ready for you, and he wasn't there."

Not waiting to hear more, I run full tilt to Northstar's stall, hoping to find him there. Hoping to find that this is all a big misunderstanding. Ash catches up to me with a couple of long strides and encircles my waist with one strong arm, pulling me back against his chest. But not before I see Gus throwing fresh hay on Northstar's stall floor.

"What happened, Gus?" I cry out. "Where's Northstar?"

Gus looks over my shoulder at Ash.

"Stop looking at Ash and talk to me!" It's then that I notice the blood on the floor. "No. No." I would have dropped to my knees if Ash had not been holding me up.

I don't notice Dr. Morrison until he comes to stand beside Ash and me. "Northstar hasn't been missing that long. Probably only since early this morning. And the blood looks much worse than it actually is. That amount of blood loss is not enough to kill him. Someone has taken him, but he's most likely still alive. He's very, very rare. And valuable. He's worth much more alive than dead. Someone may want him for their private collection or as a stud. Someone could make a fortune from his bloodline. Or . . ."

"Or what?" I'm numb, unable to look away from the blood.

"He may have been taken to be ransomed back to you." Dr. Morrison's voice is neutral and pragmatic.

"Does the Queen know?" I ask no one in particular.

"She's aware," Ash responds.

Thank the gods. Despite our adversarial relationship, I know she won't let this go unanswered. Whoever came into her territory and took Northstar made a grave mistake. And I mean *grave*. No one steals from the Queen and lives to tell the tale. She's a killer. An apex predator that always gets her man. *And one day, her power will be mine. I wish that day were today.*

The first time I saw her kill, I was ten years old. She'd invited her Earthside leaders—all shifters—and high-ranking humans from her territory to a dinner party on Avalon. The occasion was to recognize top performers and reward them for their great work. It was black tie, with champagne flowing and caviar on ice.

The Queen moved among the various groups as they all vied for her favor. Most of them seemed nervous and talked too loudly, asking her questions so she would stop and chat. Flattering her. Anything to catch and hold her attention.

Toward the end of the evening, she stood under a spotlight in the center of the room with a microphone, telling funny stories, entertaining the crowd and handing out awards. I'd adored my mother in those days, and watched fascinated as she held court, desperately wanting to have her charm and grace.

After she'd handed out the last award, she said, "We have one more item on the agenda tonight. Malcolm Trent, can you come up here please." It was not a question.

One of her leaders, a muscle-bound wolf shifter, stood up from a table way in the back and made his way slowly to the front of the room.

"Malcolm here has been a naughty boy," the Queen said, smiling at the room while she walked a circle around Malcolm. "Very naughty."

Malcolm lifted his hands slightly and started to say something, but the Queen cut him off. "So naughty in fact he thought he could steal from me and I'd never notice."

Standing under the spotlight, she turned her gaze on him. "Malcolm, you've made some terrible mistakes. Mistakes that are going to cost you dearly." With the microphone in one hand, she pointed the other at Malcolm.

I swung my gaze to Malcolm as his hands flew to his neck. He gasped for breath as he scratched and gouged frantically at his own skin, trying to break the invisible grip.

She stood there, looking out at the audience and recounting Malcolm's transgressions, all the while choking the life from his body. From time to time, she'd release her hold on him, giving him hope and a chance to breathe, only to retighten her grip. She *toyed* with him.

When he was dead, the Queen stood over his body with a glass of champagne in her hand. "To Malcolm," she said evenly, "may his mistakes be a lesson to all." She looked directly at me as she sipped her drink.

Everyone in that room, except me, lifted their glass and drank. I just stared. Not shocked, not appalled, most certainly not scared. I was mesmerized by her power. Even as a little girl, I'd understood her message loud and clear. *Fuck with the Queen and pay the ultimate price.*

CHAPTER TWENTY

TOO HEARTBROKEN AT NORTHSTAR'S disappearance to move, I stand silently in the stables for a long time. Long after Dr. Morrison has left and Gus has cleaned out Northstar's stall. Ash has stayed as well. He's leaning up against a stall a few feet away, quietly chewing on a single blade of yellow straw.

Ash pulls the straw out of his mouth and throws it to the ground before coming to stand in front of me. He reaches out tentatively, and rests his hands on my shoulders. When I don't pull away, he steps toward me and gently places his arms around me. In my misery, I let him. "You heard what Dr. Morrison said. Northstar is most likely alive somewhere. We're going to find him. We're going to get him back. And Steel and Silver are doing much better today. We're going to get all of this sorted out."

Yes, Dr. Morrison is "cautiously optimistic" about how the boys are responding to treatment for what he now firmly believes is poisoning, accidental or otherwise. He's going to keep them in the stables for another day or two, but he's expecting them to make a full recovery.

This good news does nothing to diminish the anguish I feel at the thought of someone hurting and kidnapping Northstar. How badly is he injured? Is he being cared for? Who has him? Where is he? Is he scared? The not knowing is twisting my stomach into tight knots.

Upon hearing the news about Northstar, I became numb, as if all my emotions went into a deep freeze. The heat of Ash's body is thawing me out, and a sense of being trapped, like a net is closing around me, replaces my numbness. And that trapped feeling has my fight-or-flight response kicking in.

I lift my chin and pin Ash with a flinty stare. He runs his hands lightly up and down my back, but I will not be soothed. My voice is thick with rage when I say, "I can't help but notice that my life has gone to *shit* since you got here. First, I'm ordered home from school and don't graduate."

Ash's hands still on my back. "I didn't know you didn't graduate. I thought you'd finish online. I'm sorry about that."

I'm not interested in his half-assed apologies. "Then I lose Nicky-"

He sets his jaw and interrupts me. "Princess, I know you're upset—"

I interrupt him right back. "And then I'm forced into a marriage with you."

"Forced?" His eyebrows raise over wide eyes.

"Yes, Ashton, forced! What would you call it?" I ask, my tone venomous.

He releases me and takes several long strides away before turning around to face me. "Yes, it's an arranged marriage, and I know you were surprised and reluctant at first, but you signed on the dotted line and went through with the binding ceremony. And I've had opportunities to *force* the issue—to consummate this marriage—and I didn't take them. Or have you conveniently forgotten about the morning we almost had sex in your bed." He runs his hand through this hair and gives me an intense stare.

I ignore his comment. "Then Steel and Silver are poisoned." I snap my arm out and point a rigid finger toward Northstar's stall. "And now this!" My eyes shoot daggers at him. "It's all a little too coincidental, don't you think?" Could Ash have done these things? How much do I really know about him?

Ash concentrates on a spot on the floor a few feet in front of him. Then he lifts his piercing eyes to mine. "Are you fucking serious right now? You think I had something to do with this? You honestly think I'd poison your dogs or hurt Northstar?"

"Where were you this morning?"

"In the office. Not that I should have to justify myself to you."

"Did anyone see you?"

"Yes," he grinds out. "And in case I have to say the words, which apparently I do, I didn't have anything to do with this."

Suddenly, I'm very tired of playing games with Ash. I turn and walk away from him, needing some space.

"You're awfully quick to paint me as the enemy. I know you've spent most of your life in this gilded cage and have very little experience with the outside world or the people in it, but I'm not the bad guy here."

Stopping momentarily, I glance over my shoulder at him. "I don't know what you are, Ash." And that's the truth.

The next day, I walk into our office and find Ash bent over some paperwork at his desk. He lifts his head when I enter but doesn't smile. Storm clouds fill his eyes, and his lips are compressed in a tight line. Without so much as a nod of acknowledgment, he goes back to work.

Although I don't particularly want to see him, I'm not going to hide out in my apartment, either. It's clear to me now there's some kind of game afoot. First, Ash shows up on my doorstep after fifteen years with no contact, then the Queen marries me off to him within a week, and now someone is hurting the things I love most. Then there are the nightmares of being pursued by an unknown male. I never had them until Ash arrived, and now they're tormenting me. Last night, I woke up so scared I had to turn my bedroom light on and couldn't relax enough to go back to sleep.

I spy my violet on Ash's desk. "What's my plant doing over there?"

He looks up from the papers he's been studying. "She likes it. Closer to the window."

Adjusting my black-knit bodycon dress, I sit down in my chair, leaving my plant where it is.

Ash tosses the papers across his desk. "Since New York, have you had any more power flickers? Any further signs that your power might be coming in?"

My nonexistent power. He couldn't have brought up a more tender topic. "Why are you asking about my magic? I swear, you're worse than the Queen."

"I'm concerned about you, Princess. There are some strange things happening at your court. We would all rest easier if you had your power."

"Oh, yes, that's right. That's why you married me. To get your hands on the Queen's power. And let's not forget about her Earthside territory."

"Thank you for reminding me of your attributes. I'd completely forgotten you had any." The storm clouds in his eyes have darkened into thunder clouds.

Now he's just being intentionally hurtful. *Well, two can play that game.* "Know who didn't care about power or territory? Nicky. He just wanted me for me."

"Just wanted you for you? Knowing how power hungry the Rossi family is, I find that hard to believe. The more I think about it, the more I question what his true motivations were."

"I should be married to him, not you. And if I could annul this marriage, I would." *Should I be married to Nicky? I don't know anymore.*

This conversation has gone downhill fast, and I'm too tired to deal with Ash today. Stomping out of the office is childish, but I can't seem to help myself. Ash brings out my stomping side.

Halfway to the door, I feel him hot on my trail. His hands shoot out, and he grabs my shoulders. Spinning me around to face him, he leans down so we're nose to nose.

"Another thing I'm getting tired of is you walking away from me every time I say something you don't like. The only time I should see your back, Princess, is when I'm fucking you from behind."

Then his mouth is on mine in a bruising open-mouthed kiss that makes my knees weak. His full lips press almost violently against mine, and his hand on the back of my neck slides up into my hair. Before I can stop myself, I'm returning the kiss. His tongue explores the inside of my mouth, showing me who's in charge, making my nipples tighten and my body tingle wherever it's in contact with his.

His free hand captures my breast in a firm caress over the thin fabric of my dress and bra. He rolls my overly sensitive nipple between his thumb and index finger and lust like I've never experienced courses through me. Instantly, my breasts swell, and a sweet ache blooms in my core.

Kissing me more gently, Ash bends down slightly to pull up the short skirt of my dress and move my panties to the side in one deft motion.

Spreading my legs, I give him better access to where I want his touch most. The pad of his thumb finds my clit and currents of ecstasy radiate through me as he rubs the sensitive bundle of nerves. His thumb slides down to my entrance and into my gathering wetness before massaging my clit again.

I tilt my hips forward in a needy motion, and when he inserts the tip of his index finger inside me, I explode. Coming apart with almost no warning, I cry out into his mouth as my entire body convulses in orgasm. He continues to play with me until he wrings out every last tremor from my body.

When he pulls his hand from between my legs and abruptly releases me, I sway limply, wanting only to be back in his arms. It's as if he's awakened a hunger buried deep within my body that demands to be fed. "I want you, Ash." The words fall without thought from my lips, but they're true.

Ash steps back and sucks on the finger that's just been inside me, the look in his eyes ferocious and conflicted. "You don't know what you want. Tomorrow you'll say I seduced you, forced you to do something you weren't ready to do. Ask me again when you're not in a post-orgasm dopamine fog, and I'll be more than happy to fuck you."

With my pussy still throbbing and my brain in orgasm town, I stand there with my dress askew, silently begging him with my wide eyes and kiss-swollen lips to give me what I want.

"Do you have any idea how hard it is to say no when you look at me like that? Princess, it's confirmed. You *are* going to be the fucking death of me," he says before stalking out of the office without a backward glance.

CHAPTER TWENTY-ONE

I'M IN MY ROOM, putting in a pair of diamond stud earrings, when Kat walks in, her face unsmiling. "Nina, we need to talk."

"Is it about Northstar? Or the boys?" I instantly turn to face her, my voice strained and my eyes bleary from another night of the silhouetted male pursuing me through the shadows of my dreams.

"No, sorry. There's nothing on Northstar. And as far as I know, the boys are fine."

I turn back around and face the mirror. "I'm getting ready for work. Can this wait?" I haven't heard anything from Ash since I asked him to have sex with me yesterday and he said no. The half of me containing a brain is thankful we didn't consummate the marriage. The other half of me is annoyed and frustrated. I need to get my game face on before I see him.

"I think we'd better talk before you see Ash. Come on out to the living room when you're dressed."

This sounds serious, and I'm not sure how much more drama I can take. I swipe on some mascara and give my lips a sheen of gloss. Performing the everyday tasks of getting ready helps settle my churning stomach.

In the living room, I find Kat pacing behind my couch and Gia sitting on a side chair, twirling the end of a lock of hair.

"Okay, what's going on?"

Kat stops and fixes her gaze on me. "I think you better sit down."

I walk over to the couch and perch on the edge, my back ramrod straight.

Kat joins me on the couch and sits facing me. "Some new information has come to light. I have some good news and some bad news. Which do you want first?"

"Can we start with the good news? I could really use some of that right now."

"The investigators turned up something on Ash." Kat sits back and folds her hands in her lap. "Something big. Something that, if it's true, we could use to break his contract and annul the marriage."

This is the good news? Yes, this is good news. I don't want to be married to Ash, I remind myself. "Spit it out. Tell me what you found."

"It seems he was accused of killing his roommate when he was at the University of Melbourne. In his first year. It looks like his father intervened, and it was covered up. I've reviewed his marriage contract several times. There's no mention of this charge."

Killing is common. It happens all the time. That isn't the issue, The issue is failing to disclose a murder charge. The marriage contract includes the question, "Have you ever been charged with a capital offense on any plane? If yes, provide the details." By not including the murder charge in the marriage contract, he'd misrepresented his character, and this is grounds for an annulment.

I think about Ash's tattoos. The one on his left shoulder. The one he said he'd gotten for his first kill.

I clear my throat. "You said, *if* it turned out to be true. Don't we know if it's true?"

"The investigators are still talking to people," Kat explains. "It's been difficult to find anyone who'll talk about it. Who'll speak against Ash and the Mountcastle family. They wield a lot of influence. But this is a very promising development."

"Yes, I guess it is. Let me know as soon as you find out anything more." Why would he lie on the contract? What's he hiding?

Gia and Kat make meaningful eye contact, and I feel the atmosphere in the room change, becoming rife with unease. Then Gia says, "And now for the bad news. It's about the Queen. And Ash."

"Can you two stop with all the dramatic pauses, please. Just tell me already." I'm tired of all the dancing around. As a matter of fact, I'm just plain tired.

Kat keeps her voice neutral and seems to carefully choose her words. "We have reason to believe the Queen approached Ash about marrying you. Not the other way around."

I look from Kat to Gia. Then back to Kat, my stomach in knots. "What are you talking about? What did you hear?"

"As part of our investigation on Ash, we discovered that he attended a meeting Earthside, in Melbourne, with his father and the Queen. The meeting took place in early April."

"That doesn't prove anything," I scoff, not wanting to think about the Queen offering me to Ash as if I were chattel. Acid roils in my stomach.

Gia comes and sits beside me on the couch. "The timing of the meeting would have been after Nicky submitted his offer of marriage and just before Ash showed up here, completely out of the blue, I might add, with *his* offer."

I don't want this to be true. It's bad enough the Queen accepted Ash's contract without talking to me first, but if she had asked him, or worse, commanded him to marry me, I would be humiliated. My abdomen cramps painfully at the thought.

"I don't remember the Queen saying anything about a trip to Australia. Are you sure it was her that he met with?" Thankfully, my voice is rock steady and doesn't betray how much this hurts.

"I had my weekly meeting with the Queen's press secretary early this morning and casually brought it up. She confirmed the Queen had made a last-minute trip to Melbourne in April." Gia's big blue eyes shine with sympathy. She knows my hard outer shell masks my soft interior filled with insecurity and that I'll be mortified if this is true.

"It could all be a coincidence. He said he wanted to marry me because his dragon chose me," I say, barely able to breathe. *Was that a lie, too?* I know he has his eye on the Queen's power and Earthside territory—he told me that himself. But I also thought he cared about me at least a little because I'm his so-called fated mate. And even though I fought hard against it, I've started to care about him, too. I would've slept with him yesterday.

"I thought you didn't believe in this fated mate business. Either way, I don't like it," Kat states bluntly. "The timing seems a little too convenient."

Hadn't I just said something similar to Ash?

"You should talk to the Queen," Kat says decisively.

CHAPTER
TWENTY-TWO

"I NEED TO SEE the Queen, Stew." I try not to let any distress show on my face.

"I'm sorry. I don't see you in her calendar, princess." Stewart sits behind his desk outside the Queen's office, pretending to look at her schedule, which he has committed to memory and knows damn well I'm not on.

"I don't have an appointment," I say, breezing past him. When I reach the doors of her office, two members of the Gorm step in front of me.

"Let the princess pass," Stewart says without hesitation.

He must see I'm on a mission.

After opening the doors, the guards move aside and I walk into the office. The Queen and her consort look up at me from a tea table where they are working.

"Princess Seraphina, what is the purpose of this interruption?" the consort asks. "The Queen and I are busy. Run along."

The consort and I tolerate each other because he's married to my mother, but we're not friends. Ever since I can remember, he's never missed an opportunity to make me feel small and unimportant. "I would like to have a word with the Queen. Alone."

"Princess, anything you have to say to the Queen, you can say in front of me." The consort gives me a patronizing smile.

"You may leave us." The Queen dismisses him with her patented wave.

With his bland features pinched into a scowl, the consort leaves without a word.

The Queen gestures with an outstretched hand that I should take a seat. I do, and feel the warm flow of her power feather across my skin.

She folds her hands in her lap, her cream blouse neatly tucked into a red pencil skirt. Her hair is down and tucked behind one ear; her makeup is understated and flawless. She appears pleasant and approachable.

This is an illusion that doesn't fool me for a second.

"I am glad you're here, actually," she begins. "I wanted to inform you that the Gorm is searching the island and questioning everyone, not only for clues about Northstar, but also to locate the substance that poisoned Steel and Silver. I personally made inquiries into Northstar's disappearance and have trusted contacts out looking for him on every plane. And I have invited the visiting Spanish jaguars to remain on Avalon until we have more answers. Thiago wanted my support in a bid to take over Portugal and kill its current leader. I denied his request, of course. As a member of the Council of Seven, I cannot be getting involved in these petty squabbles over territory."

Invited means she is not letting the jaguar shifters leave Avalon in case they had something to do with Northstar's kidnapping. She's holding them hostage. I don't second-guess her methods. I want the safe return of Northstar that badly.

"Thank you. I appreciate that you're doing everything possible to find him. Are the guards going to question Ash as well?"

The Queen blinks at me, looking taken aback by my question. "They are talking to everyone. Is there anything else on your mind, Princess?"

"Yes, actually. I just heard some rather distressing news." I put my emotions back in the deep freeze in preparation for whatever this conversation might reveal.

"Oh, really. What is that?" The Queen glances at her Patek Philippe wristwatch.

"That you made an unscheduled trip Earthside to Australia, right after Nicky offered for me and right before Ash did. That you commanded Ash to marry me." I hold my breath.

"And where did you hear this?" Her tone is deceptively gentle, but her power skitters over me so I don't forget it's there.

"It doesn't matter. Is it true?" My voice doesn't hold a single note of the fury I've locked away.

"I did not *command* him to offer for you. But even if I did, what is the problem? This is an arranged marriage. What difference does it make how it was arranged?"

"It matters to me. If you didn't *command* him, did you bribe him with something? Did you buy me a husband?"

"I would not use the word *buy.*"

Her power changes from a rippling flow to pinpricks on my arms and face, as if I'm being pelted by stinging drops of hard rain. "What word would you use then? Procure?" I tilt my head to the side, feigning innocent interest. "Is that what you are? A *procurer?*" My emotions, too strong to hold back, rise up to the surface. My anger is a deep and quiet entity in the room. I'm tired of being a pawn.

"I do not owe you an explanation for my actions. Anything I choose to share with you is a courtesy. Not a necessity. Do not forget which one of us is Queen." She uses her power to push me back against my chair.

I attempt to find my magic, to push her right back, but nothing happens. I have never wanted my own power so badly. The look on her face would be worth whatever consequences I would face after.

"I will tell you this. You need Ashton, whether you know it or not. This court needs him. One day, you will be Queen and you will need his strength. I did what was best for everyone, including you."

CHAPTER
TWENTY-THREE

I LEAVE THE QUEEN'S office because I won't be getting any more information from her. She may not have said the words outright, but what she did say was stinging confirmation of my worst fear. There was a deal, a bargain struck between her and Ash. *He never cared about me.*

Storming into the office Ash and I share, I slam the door behind me. "Is there something you want to tell me?" I demand, noticing my violet is still on his desk.

"Door slamming, shouting and accusations. The Princess must have decided to grace me with her presence. What am I supposed to have done now?" His face is like granite. His twinkling eyes and teasing grin are nowhere to be seen.

"For once since you got here, be honest." I won't be intimidated by his stony demeanor.

"Why don't you slow down and tell me what the fuck you're talking about."

I stride across the office and stand right in front of his desk with my arms crossed. "I know you and your father met with the Queen in Melbourne right before you showed up here with a marriage contract in hand." I decided on the walk over to our office not to bring up the murder he was accused of while at university. I don't want to tip my hand while we're still looking into it.

"Yes. And. So what?" His words are clipped, his tone nothing but displeasure.

"You might as well tell me the truth. The Queen has already told me everything." This is not exactly true, but I want answers.

He leans forward, resting his elbows on his desk. "Yes, the Queen requested a meeting. And yes, my father and I met with her. But like you already know, my dragon had decided, for better or worse, that you are his fated mate." Ash's face hardens even more as he says this last bit.

I can't confirm his fated-mate claim, though I really wish I could. I have to focus on the facts. "Let's cut to the chase. What did she give you to marry me?" I feel like such a fool for having to ask this question. I can barely breathe, waiting for his response. His answer has the potential to hurt me so deeply. Somewhere along the line, his motivation for marrying me and how he feels about me have become very important.

"Nothing." He never breaks eye contact with me. He doesn't even blink.

"Did she pay you in cash? Promise you territory? Jewels? Power? What sealed the deal for you?" I ask angrily.

"I told you. She didn't offer me anything, and I didn't ask for anything. There's nothing your mother has that I want."

Placing my hands on his desk, I look him directly in the eye. "You once told me you weren't my newest toy. Well, let me *tell you* something, she bought you as sure as she bought all my other pets."

"I'm starting to lose my patience with you, Princess. Okay, you want the unvarnished truth? Here it is. My father and I did meet with your mother. And yes, she did want to arrange a marriage between you and me to align our families. She wanted to protect her court, her legacy, and you. You know there have been threats against her and at least one assassination attempt." Ash exhales slowly. "The threats are now directed at you, too."

My head snaps back in shock. "No one told me there'd been threats made against me. Why in the hell didn't anyone tell me?"

"Your mother didn't want you to know. She thought if she told you, you'd think she was exaggerating the threat, using it as leverage to control you. She worried if she tightened your security or forbade you to leave Avalon, you'd rebel and do something reckless. Having gotten to know you, I'm not surprised she felt that way. You're impulsive and impetuous."

Impulsive? Impetuous? "So, nobody thought it might be a good idea to tell *me* about the threats? Nobody thought this is information *I* might need to fucking know? And why didn't *you* tell me about the fact you met with the Queen before you came to Avalon? That's how you heard about Nicky's contract, isn't it?"

"Your mother told my father about Nick's contract when she requested the meeting, and my father told me. I didn't lie to you when I said I heard about it from my parents. I was already planning to come to your court. If you remember, I was trying to get in touch with you. But Nick's contract and the threats against you hurried up my time line in coming to Avalon." Ash leans forward and rests his forearms on his desk. "Your mother thought it would be wise not to tell you she'd come to see me first. That it would only make the marriage more difficult for you to accept. That we should focus on the fact my dragon had chosen you and leave it at that." Ash reclines back in his chair and steeples his fingers. "And the first time I met you, I had to agree with her thinking. You were so angry with her, you could barely talk. You didn't even look at me. You didn't reject me—you rejected her choice, her interference. You've held on to that anger every day since, using it as a weapon against me. And honestly, if you could put aside your mommy complex for two minutes, you'd be able to see that."

Mommy complex? Fuck that. He knows nothing about my relationship with her. "Here's some honesty for you," I say tightly. "I don't want to be bound to you, and I will *never* willingly consummate this marriage. I can't stand the sight of you."

Ash shoots out of his chair and slaps his hands down on his desk, eyes gleaming. "Just yesterday, I had you wet and willing in this very office. You came in my arms and practically begged me to fuck you. I could've lifted your dress, bent you over this desk and consummated this marriage right here." Ash taps his desk in emphasis. "I could've put all this fucking foolishness behind us. You can lie to me, Princess. But don't lie to yourself."

"I still have a trick or two up my sleeve, and I'll be getting that annulment."

"You're acting like a brat." He straightens to his full height and points a finger at me. "You signed that contract, and you'll be fulfilling it."

"Like fuck I will." I see red.

"I should take you over my knee and spank some sense into you. Wake up, Princess. I'm the only one willing to tell you the truth. If you let me in, I'll be your friend."

"You've been having backroom meetings with the Queen, making decisions about my life without including me and withholding information from me since you got here. With friends like you Ash, I don't need enemies."

I call Kat the minute I leave the office; my heart pounding out of my chest.

"Nina," she answers immediately, her tone brisk.

"Did you know? My voice is a breathy whisper. "Did you know there were threats against me?"

Silence.

"Kat?"

"I didn't know anything concrete, but I had my suspicions. There were some rumors around the castle that you were receiving threats, too. Violent ones. When the Queen summoned you home from school early, I reached out to her lawyers to find out if it was true. The Queen's lawyers said they could neither confirm nor deny."

"Why didn't you tell me?" I'm incredulous.

"Because I had no proof. It was all conjecture and hearsay. I shared my suspicions with Sofie and Gia, and together we decided it would probably be best not to tell you yet."

"Why not?"

"Because, Nina, we know you. You'd think the Queen planted the threats as a way to keep you on Avalon. And you tend to freak out when you feel like you're being controlled or managed."

"You should've told me," I say right before ending the call. Even my best friends are keeping me in the dark.

CHAPTER
TWENTY-FOUR

I NEED TO FIND some peace, and the one place I've always been able to do that is in the stables. Slipping into my most comfortable riding clothes and pulling on a pair of well-loved boots, I think about Northstar. My heart constricts at the thought that he won't be there. That he's still missing. That someone has taken him from his home and everything he knows.

As I approach the white limestone stables, my shoulders fall away from my ears, and I'm able to relax a little for the first time in days. The stress over Northstar and my dogs, the nightmares, the betrayal by Ash and my friends, it's all too much. I expect duplicity from the Queen, but from the others, it hurts. And now I also have the threats against me to worry about.

But the familiar sight of the grooms walking horses in and out of the arched entryways and the smell of clean hay soothes me. I stand there for a minute, close my eyes and breathe it all in, feeling the fight go out of me.

"I need to talk to you." Ash's deep voice disturbs my tranquility.

"I'm not sure we have a lot left to say to each other," I say quietly, glancing at him briefly before walking into the stables. Inside, I find a groom brushing the shiny coat of an Arabian named Black Opal. He's one of the Queen's favorites.

"I'll take over for you if you don't mind," I say to the groom. Spending time with horses always takes me to my happy place.

"Yes, of course. I'll come back for him in twenty minutes. He's got his checkup with Dr. Morrison."

I nod in agreement. The groom hands me the brush and with a small bow turns and leaves.

Black Opal stands proudly, his long neck extended, his head held at an angle that exudes confidence and nobility. I begin gently brushing down his shoulder and flank as I flick my eyes to Ash over Black Opal's back, the horse acting as a barrier between us. "What do you want, Ash?"

Ash stands tall and proud, exuding his own form of confidence and nobility. "My father called me today. Let me know that some investigators have been asking questions about me Earthside. About my time at university. Would you happen to know anything about that?"

"Yes, as a matter of fact, I do. Those investigators were hired by Kat on my behalf." I stop brushing Black Opal and meet Ash's eyes, deciding to put all my cards on the table. "I know you were accused of murdering your roommate, and your father covered it up. You never included this murder charge in your marriage contract. And that's grounds for an annulment." In the impassioned heat of an argument with Ash, it's easy for me to get swept up and run my mouth. But standing here in the serene atmosphere of the stables, I have to ask myself, *Is an annulment really what I want?*

"You don't know anything, Nina, and those investigators must be unprofessional amateurs." Ash's voice is composed and even, but his set jaw and rigid body give away his agitation. "My first-year roommate committed suicide. His parents were distraught and wanted someone to blame. I was convenient. Everybody knew I was a shifter. The Earthside police talked to me a couple of times, but never arrested me. My parents didn't cover it up because I was never formally charged."

I lower my eyes to Black Opal's flank and return to brushing him as he nickers softly. *Is that relief I feel?*

"Even though I wasn't arrested, that was an extremely difficult time for me." Ash runs his hands through his hair. "Being falsely accused of murder changes you. It makes you very aware of how valuable your name and integrity are. And how quickly they can both be destroyed. There were rumors and untrue stories about me afterward. Everybody assumed I did it because I'm a shifter. People were afraid of me. Nobody wants to get a beer or go to a rugby game with a murderer. Do you have any idea what it's like to be feared for something you didn't do? Hated for what you are? I could have easily left and started over again at a new school, but I stayed to prove the gossips wrong. And after about a year, everybody began to realize I had nothing to do with his death and I was slowly able to put it behind me. I haven't thought about it in a long time. Until now."

Ash takes a deep breath and exhales slowly. "I know I didn't tell you about meeting your mother or the threats against you. But I was trying to protect you." Ash fixes me with a somber gaze. "And since coming to your court, I've made my intentions toward you perfectly clear. I have never played games with you. Can you say the same? I don't think you can. Well, I'm tired of your games, and I'm *done* having my honor called into question by you. Your trust issues are just that. *Yours*."

The finality in his deep voice causes me to break out in a cold sweat and the hair on the back of my neck to stand up. I watch silently as Ash walks away from me and out of the stables.

What have I done? The sting of tears pricks my eyes as I watch Ash walk away. But under no circumstances will I chase after him or stand in the stables crying like a little girl.

Instead, I blink back the tears and mechanically brush Black Opal until the groom comes back for him.

I spend a couple more hours working with the horses and doing small chores around the stables, trying to make sense of the last few weeks of my life and realizing that I may have fallen for Ash despite my best efforts not to. Did he mean it when he said he was done? Did I push him too far? Anxious adrenaline skips through me. *Don't panic. You're married. He's not going anywhere.* I take a deep breath. *There's still time.*

I'm sitting at my desk later that day waiting to talk to Ash when my phone rings. Picking it up, I'm hoping to see his name on my screen, but it's Kat.

Before I can even get out a hello, she shouts triumphantly, "You've won!"

"What're you talking about?"

"You've won. Ash's lawyer, Luke, just called me. They're filing for an annulment."

I instantly double over as if someone punched me in the stomach and knocked the air out of me. He's breaking the marriage contract. "I need to talk to Ash," I say breathlessly.

"He's not here. He left Avalon earlier today. Went back to New York. You didn't know?"

He's gone. My heart explodes into a million sharp pieces like the glass of a shattered window.

"Nina, are you there? This is what you wanted, right?" Kat sounds confused, and I don't blame her. Even I don't know what I want anymore.

I take a long time to answer as I learn how to breathe around the pain in my chest. "Yeah. I mean, yes, definitely." I try not to let the tears welling up in my eyes be heard in my voice. I clear my throat. "On what grounds?"

"I don't have the paperwork yet, but Luke hinted at lack of consummation. I'm assuming that's correct?"

"Yes, Ash and I never had sex." I think back to all the opportunities I'd had to consummate our marriage. Why hadn't I taken them?

"Well, it worked. I can't believe it, but it worked. Congratulations, you outlasted him, Nina. I'll call you back when the paperwork arrives. Oh, wait, before I forget. That thing about Ash being accused of murder when he was in university—it turned out to be a red herring. There was nothing to the story. Fucking incompetent investigators. Not that it matters now."

"No, it doesn't matter now," I say before ending the call. I won. So why is my heart breaking? With blurry vision, I notice the violets sitting on my desk. *He's really gone.*

I don't know how long I sit there looking at the violets, thinking about Ash. It could have been thirty seconds; it could have been three hours. Time has stopped.

I pick up my phone and display my camera roll, looking for the pictures of Ash and me from New York. Scrolling through them, I relive the memories and wish I could go back in time.

To the moment Ash threw his arm around me and held me close in Grand Central Terminal.

Or when we burst out laughing, all bright eyes and big smiles, on the Staten Island Ferry.

Then I find our wedding picture. The one Ash asked Ben to take and post online, announcing to the planes we were husband and wife.

Seeing our wedding photo causes the painful ache in my chest to expand as if all the broken pieces of my heart are now bloody shrapnel in my lungs. I rest my forehead on my desk, trying and failing to pull myself together.

My phone rings, and without looking, I press it to my ear, expecting it's Kat calling back about the annulment. "Hello," I answer quietly.

"Ciao, Bella."

I sit straight up. I'd know that voice anywhere. Then I remember the owner of that voice has completely ghosted me. I grit my teeth. "Hello, Nicky. Nice of you to get back to me. Finally." I channel all of my brokenhearted devastation over Ash into cold rage at Nicky.

"I know I have some explaining to do, Bella." His voice is silky.

"You're fucking right you do. It's been weeks. I sent you a thousand texts. I called you a thousand times." My level of pissed off plain in my voice.

"We need to talk. But not over the phone. Can you come here? I'm back in Providence. Packing up some pieces for a show."

"Why should I?" But I already know I'm going to see him. Something inside me compels me to.

"If you ever cared for me, you'll come. I really need to see you," he says, his tone cajoling and persuasive.

I don't say anything for a long time. Let him wait. "Fine, I'll meet you at your place tonight."

"See you soon, Bella. Ciao."

I end the call and send a text to the girls in our group chat to meet me back in my apartment. I'm going to need their help getting off this island without alerting the Queen.

CHAPTER TWENTY-FIVE

"I DON'T THINK THIS is a good idea," Sofie says, tapping her index finger on her chin thoughtfully.

Kat nods her head. "I agree with Sofie. I don't like this. Why does Nicky want to see you now?"

"It's been complete radio silence from him for weeks. Almost a month actually." Gia makes it three for three against me going to see him.

"I know," I say. "He said he wants a chance to talk. To explain." Fresh from the shower and blow-drying my hair, I'm wearing a short, pink satin robe as I hunt through my closet, searching for the perfect outfit. Something that doesn't look like I'm trying too hard. I decide on dark-wash jeans, heeled boots and a heather gray sweater.

Walking over to my dresser, I open the top drawer. After perusing the contents for a minute, I choose a black lace thong, a push-up bra and a black cami. I let my robe drop to the floor, not caring that the girls are here, and slip into my underthings.

"Are you going to talk to Nicky, or are you going to fuck him?" Gia asks.

"Maybe both." I shimmy into my tight jeans and pull on my sweater. "If everyone thinks I'm so . . . what did Ash call me? Oh, that's right, *impulsive* and *impetuous.* Maybe I should live up to my reputation." I'm not really planning to have sex with Nicky. I'm devastated over Ash. And besides, Nicky is on my shit list for ghosting me. I just need to hear what he has to say.

"And what about Ash?" Sofie asks carefully.

I stop what I'm doing and look at Kat, my breath coming fast and shallow. "Didn't you tell them about the annulment?"

"Yes, I told them," Kat replies. "Listen, I know you want to talk to Nicky, but what's the rush? Take a few days. Sort out your obviously conflicted feelings about Ash before doing anything."

"Ash is annulling our marriage." It crushes me to say the words aloud. "*I think*"—I use sarcasm to cover up my pain—"we're broken up. There's nothing left to sort out."

"This thing with you and Ash." Sofie's fretful eyes hold mine. "It's been complicated. But I think he cares about you, Nina. And I know you care about him."

I open my mouth to say that I don't care about him, but there's no use lying to this group. They'd know. But I don't want to talk about Ash anymore. It hurts too much. "Ash made his decision. And I have to see Nicky tonight. He's back in Providence, and the Queen has left the island for a Council of Seven meeting. This is my chance to leave without her knowing." I sit on a padded bench in my dressing area and slide on my ankle boots.

Once you're on Avalon, the Queen can not only keep you here, but she can track your magic to see where you go when you leave. I'm hoping the Queen is distracted enough by her meeting not to notice someone's left Avalon. And if she does notice, I'm hoping my use of the girls' power will make her think it's one of them.

Grabbing my oversized black Birkin bag, I say, "I'm going to need some help getting out of here." I stare expectantly at each of them.

They all look anywhere but at me.

"Has everyone forgotten Nicky and I were engaged? And that our engagement ended because of the Queen and not because of a decision either of us made? I owe it to Nicky to talk to him. And more importantly, I owe it to myself. Please help me." *I have to do this.*

"What do you want us to do?" Gia asks, still looking unsure.

"Jump me back to Brown. East campus entrance," I say.

The girls exchange a quick look and then encircle me, holding hands. There is a flash of light, and the next thing I know, I'm back on campus, a stone's throw away from Nicky's place.

CHAPTER TWENTY-SIX

I GATHER MY THOUGHTS on the short walk from campus to Nicky's place. The last time I saw him, almost a month ago, we'd been making plans for a future together as husband and wife. Now, I'm three weeks into a marriage with Ash. A marriage I just learned is about to be annulled. How has my life gotten so out of hand?

Strolling up the front steps to Nicky's red brick Victorian, a wave of anxiety hits me, as if being here isn't such a good idea. I shake off my internal warning system. *It's Nicky, for goodness sake. You're just nervous walking alone in the dark.* Taking a steadying breath in the dim light of the porch, I give the front door a quick knock and walk in without waiting.

"In the studio," Nicky yells from the back of the house.

Dropping my Birkin bag on a small table in the entryway, the familiar routine eases my nerves. The house feels so familiar, smells so familiar. It's as if Nicky and I have never been apart. *What was I so worried about?*

My boots herald my approach, and when I step into his studio, he puts down the painting he's admiring and gifts me with a dazzling smile. He's beautiful. He makes a white V-neck T-shirt and well-worn jeans look like a million-dollars. And he's not even wearing shoes.

Shaking his head, he walks toward me. "Bella, I've missed you. Look at this." He takes my hand and pulls me across the room. "Remember when we painted this?" It's the canvas we painted on our first date.

I can't help but smile at the memory. "Of course, I remember. How could I forget? You said I needed to learn how to color outside the lines."

"And have you?"

"Yes, I think I have," I say softly, thinking about Ash.

Still holding my hand, he leads me around the room, and we admire his paintings. Some I recognize, others I don't. When we reach a sculpture I've never seen before, he asks, "Were you here when I worked on this?" He tilts his head from side to side.

"No, I don't think so. If you recall, Nicky, we didn't spend that much time together. You were always working. I thought you asked me here so we could talk." He has a lot of explaining to do.

He throws an arm over my shoulders and pulls me into his side. "That's not how I remember it, Bella. Not at all. I remember all of the good times we had. But you're right about one thing, we need to talk." He guides me to his kitchen, where he maneuvers around the breakfast bar, and I pull up a stool. He opens a bottle of red wine with a flourish and pours two glasses.

As he hands me a glass of wine, he asks, "Did you cut your hair? I don't like it. I prefer it longer."

My hand flies to my hair, and I wrinkle my nose at him. "I didn't cut it," I say, remembering how critical Nicky always was about my appearance.

"No need to be so sensitive, Bella."

I drop my hand. Nicky always did have a way of making me question my own emotions. *Had he ever been good for me?* "Why didn't you return any of my texts or phone calls?" I ask the question that's been haunting me for the last month.

He rubs the palms of his hands together and looks up to the ceiling before meeting my eyes. "When I found out my marriage contract had been rejected, I was humiliated."

"I didn't have anything to do with that. It was entirely the Queen's decision."

Seeming to take no notice of my comment, he continues, "Then I was called home by my father. He's working on something very important to our family, big changes in his Earthside territory. He needed my assistance." Nicky curls his lips and points a finger at me. "I thought I had more time where you were concerned. But you fucking surprised me. You married Ashton Mountcastle barely a week after my contract was rejected. I didn't plan on that. When I saw the wedding picture on Instagram, I was angry. Very angry."

"That's not how I wanted you to find out," I say. "The Queen arranged the marriage without talking to me. If you had returned my calls, I could have told you what was happening."

He comes around the breakfast bar and stands in front of me, staring intently into my eyes. After several seconds pass, he gives me a satisfied smile.

My thoughts become clouded and I find myself slipping into the dream-like state I'm often in when around him.

"Then, I was busy working for my father," Nicky says with a shrug of his shoulders. "I'm sure you can relate. You come from a royal family, too. It's duty and empire first."

I *could* relate. When the Queen called me home from school, I went without question and quickly found myself married to Ash to protect *her* legacy. "Yeah, I noticed you were busy. You totally ghosted me. You didn't fight for me at all." While my words are accusing, my tone is subdued. *Where's my anger?*

He cups my face in his hands and leans in, his lips hovering just above mine. "That's the past. Let's focus on the future. The good news is, I want you back. I want to give you another chance."

After a heartbeat, his mouth covers mine, and he's kissing me, his hands moving to my neck and up into my hair. Like his skill at painting, sculpting or even simply opening a bottle of wine, his skill at kissing is expert level. He steps between my knees, not breaking the kiss.

Why do I feel so detached? As if I'm watching him kiss me from outside my body?

Struggling to get my limbs to cooperate, I put my hand on his chest and push him back a step. "Stop. This isn't right," I say, trying to find my mental focus. "It's too late now."

"Bella . . ." His look is a combination of confused and patronizing. "What could we have done then that we can't do now? Why is it too late?"

"Because I'm married to Ash, for starters."

Nicky's eyes become sharp. "The quickest way out of that little predicament is to fuck someone else."

Adultery, unless otherwise stipulated, can be used as incontestable grounds to void a marriage contract. Of course, Nicky doesn't know Ash and I haven't consummated our marriage. He also doesn't know Ash is having the marriage annulled. "You're suggesting I break my vows, cheat on my husband?"

"I should be your husband. You should be married to me right now. I need you. My father and I have plans for you." Nicky takes my shoulders in a bruising grip.

His father? What is Nicky talking about? With great physical effort, I attempt to shrug out of his hold, but he strengthens his grip.

"And, Ash won't want you if he thinks I've had you. Trust me. Dragon shifters are known for their possessive streaks. He'll break the marriage contract as soon as he finds out."

"Let me go, Nicky." I attempt to break his hold on me again. *Why can't I muster any strength?*

"You don't understand, Bella. I can't let you go. I'm not nearly done with you."

"You're going to have to find a way. I'm not going to cheat on my husband. I made a commitment to Ash, and I'm going to honor it." *I choose Ash. I want Ash even if he doesn't feel the same about me.*

"As the husband in question, I must say, that's very good to hear." Ash's low voice fills Nicky's kitchen.

Hearing Ash's voice is like mainlining a triple shot of espresso. The fog clouding my mind clears and my sluggish muscles flex with renewed energy.

Nicky instantly releases me and takes a few steps back. With my heart in my throat, I spin to see Ash standing just inside the front door of Nicky's house, his eyes golden in the shadows. "Ash!" I squeak. "What are you doing here?"

Ash walks into the light of the kitchen. "I think the question is, what are *you* doing here, Princess?" The atmosphere in the room takes on a new, electric quality. The air is warm, scented of smoke and snaps with intensity.

My hungry eyes eat Ash up. I forget Nicky is even here.

Ash puts his large hand on the back of my neck, leans toward me and inhales deeply. Then he turns his head to nod at Nicky. "Rossi." Ash is doing that partial shift thing, letting his dragon come out a little, making him appear even bigger in the confined space of Nicky's kitchen.

"Mountcastle." Nicky nods back, allowing his own veneer of humanity to fall away. He stops pretending to breathe, his skin takes on a pale luminescence, and he curls his lips back to bare his fangs as his irises turn blood red. Nicky's power sweeps over me momentarily, like shards of ice scraping against my skin, before being replaced by the heated caress of Ash's power.

Their greeting is as deadly as it is cordial. Like two humans shaking hands before an old-fashioned duel to the death at dawn. Hot and cold energy swirl around the room as the dominance contest ratchets up. I'm scared to blink in case that tiny movement triggers the violence that's threatening in the air like a lightning strike.

Ash's eyes glow yellow, and the magic of his dragon takes over the room, suppressing Nicky's power. With the quickness of a striking cobra, Ash lunges across the kitchen and grabs Nicky by the throat. Holding Nicky off the ground, Ash's deep voice echoes around the room. "I'm only going to say this once. Stay away from my mate. Don't text her. Don't call her. Don't even think about her. If I ever find you alone with her again, I'll fucking kill you."

Nicky's fingernails elongate to talons and he attempts to slash Ash's arm and break his hold.

After what feels like an eternity but is probably only a few seconds, Ash throws Nicky across the room.

Landing on his feet, Nicky straightens his shirt and growls at Ash before swiping his glass of wine off the breakfast bar and lifting it to me in a salute. "You're making a mistake." He takes a sip of the red wine, revealing his fangs once again, a jeering glimmer in his red eyes. Then he turns and walks toward the back of the house. Halfway down the hall, he stops and pivots to face us. " You won't be able to forget me, Bella." Then he blows me a kiss.

A horrible cold burn ignites on the inside of my right thigh as if someone is stabbing me with a spike of ice. *Nicky's mark.*

In the blink of an eye, Ash is standing toe-to-toe with Nicky. Before my brain can process what's happening, Ash's big body torques, his arm shoots out, and he punches Nicky in the face several times in quick succession.

Smash. Smash. Smash.

Nicky stumbles backward and falls to the floor, a hand to his jaw.

"Get up, Rossi," Ash snarls, "so I can knock you down again."

Nicky removes his hand and I see his lower jaw hanging off his face at a sickening angle. As a vampire, he'll regenerate and recover from the broken jaw in a relatively short amount of time. I need to get Ash out of here and end this fight. I don't want Ash to kill Nicky over me.

Racing down the hall, I grab two handfuls of Ash's suit jacket. I can't physically remove him from the house, so I rely on his protective instincts to do the job for me. "Please, Ash. Get me out of here. I want to leave. Please. Let's go."

Waves of rage roll off Ash like heat off a city sidewalk on a sweaty summer day, but he takes my hand in a firm grip. As we head to the front door, I snag my bag from the entryway table.

Once we're out of the house, the pain in my thigh recedes, and I'm able to focus on what really matters. *Ash is here. He's come back to me.*

CHAPTER
TWENTY-SEVEN

O UTSIDE NICKY'S HOUSE, ASH marches me to a shiny, black BMW parked at the curb. He unlocks the car with a beep and motions for me to get into the passenger side with a jerk of his chin and a, "Get your ass in the car."

"How did you know where I was?" I'm so happy he's here, I can't take my eyes off him. *Don't get ahead of yourself. He could be here to tell you it's over.*

Ash starts the car and pulls away from the curb, keeping his eyes on the road. "I have my ways," he answers through clenched teeth, flexing his hands before reestablishing his white-knuckled grip on the steering wheel. Tension creates a thick, soupy stillness in the car.

We leave the neighborhoods surrounding the university and drive south on I-95. With each passing mile, I feel the distance between us growing and it scares me.

"Where are we going?" I ask hoping to get him to look at me, even for a second.

"The Chanler." He continues to focus straight ahead.

The Chanler is a historic mansion converted into a boutique hotel. It's perched on the Cliff Walk in Newport and is known for its breathtaking views of the Atlantic Ocean. I'm pretty sure we're not going to be checking out the views.

We make the rest of the forty-five-minute trip in silence. I use the time to think about what happened at Nicky's. What did he mean when he said his father had plans for me? Could the Queen and Ash be right, that Nicky never actually wanted me for me? That he was using me all along?

And what about the shooting pain I experienced in my thigh? It's in the exact same location as Nicky's mark. Obviously, leaving his magic hidden under the surface of my skin was a mistake. I can't tell Ash I'm still wearing Nicky's mark—it'll only make him angrier. I'll just get Sofie to remove it as soon as I get home.

Ash barely spares me a glance and doesn't speak to me as he helps me from the car, so the valet can park it, or as he checks us into the hotel.

A bellboy escorts us up to our lavish suite and shows us all the amenities—the four-poster covered bed, two-person tub, and the spectacular seascapes. After Ash sets his overnight bag into a corner and tips the bellboy, he closes the door with a click that's deafening in the glacial quiet.

When is he going to say something? I drop my bag on a nightstand and go to sit in one of the small, padded chairs in front of the windows, trying not to fidget. I don't want him to know how nervous I am.

Ash sits across from me, leaning forward with his elbows on his wide-spread knees and clasping his hands together.

Maybe so he doesn't strangle me? "How did you know where I was?" I ask again, trying to get him to talk.

"Your mother called me," Ash says, the muscles of his jawline tightening.

"Holy fuck." I guess she noticed I left Avalon.

"Yeah, that about sums it up. What the fuck were you *doing* with him?" Ash's tone is stinging, like the lash of a whip.

"Hey!" I snap, leaning forward in my chair, too. "You have no rights where I'm concerned. You filed for an annulment."

"No, I did not." He bites out each word.

"You did. Kat told me Luke called her. She said the paperwork was coming."

"I asked Luke to draw it up, but I never told him to file it."

"That's splitting hairs." I sit back in my chair, trying not to read too much into this information. "Why did you ask him to draw it up in the first place?"

"Because you accused me of poisoning your dogs, kidnapping Northstar, and plotting against you with your own mother. Not to mention, you allowed Kat to hire private investigators to dig up shit on me. Untrue shit." Ash leans back and scrubs his face with both hands. "I was fucking furious with you. I told myself to let you go. I told my dragon he was going to have to get over you. I was done."

My heart threatens to break all over again at the thought of him being done with me. I have to make him understand. "Try to see my side, Ash. You show up at my court, and my life immediately flies out of control. I'm yanked out of school and married to you within a few short days, and then someone starts hurting the things I care about most. How did I know it wasn't you trying to get back at me for not accepting the marriage? And you weren't completely honest with me. You held back on telling me you'd met with the Queen in secret prior to submitting your marriage contract and that there were threats being made against me."

"I explained to you why I felt it was better not to tell you about that meeting and the threats. The threats against you are . . . gruesome. I need to keep you safe until I can find and kill whoever is sending them. But you rebel against any form of authority, even when it's for your own good. I was trying to protect you. And I'd do it again."

Although I want to question him further about the threats, now doesn't seem like the time. I drop my eyes to the floor. The girls hadn't told me about the threats, either. And for the same reason.

"Look at me," Ash orders.

My head snaps up and I meet his hard stare, startled by the awareness that shoots through me at his commanding tone.

"You've kept me at arm's length and fought against this marriage solely because I was the Queen's choice. Well, now you have a choice to make. If you can honestly tell me you believe I'm capable of intentionally hurting you or the things you love, I'll walk out that door, and you'll never see me again. I'll give you the annulment you seem to want so badly."

I sit back in my chair and think back on the past month. The things I'd said to him. The way I'd acted. *No wonder he left.*

Ash stands and strides purposely to the door. "Goodbye, Princess."

Leaping out of my seat, I dash across the room to intercept him. Standing in front of him, I place my hands on his chest to stop him from leaving. "Please don't go. I know you're not capable of those things. I didn't know what to think at the time. You obviously didn't hurt my dogs or Northstar. You love them, and more importantly, they love you. Animals know who they can trust. I don't know why I couldn't see that." I stare earnestly into his face, trying to bridge the chasm between us. "I'm sorry I accused you of plotting against me. I was wrong about so many things."

Ash grabs my shoulders and gives me a little shake. "I almost fucking left you." Then he crushes me fiercely to him, one arm like an iron band around my back, his other hand pressing my cheek into his chest, right above his heart. I wrap my arms around him and hold on tightly as if I'll never let go.

We stand there for several minutes, both of us breathing heavily, our hearts pounding.

When he relaxes his arms a little, I pull back and look up into his eyes. "If you were letting me go, what made you come back? Was it your dragon?"

"Yes, partly. He said it isn't possible to get over you." Ash's gaze softens, becomes tender. "But the main reason I came back is that I can't seem to stay away from you. Can't seem to stop thinking about you. I missed you like crazy when I left Avalon and went back to New York." His eyes sharpen once again. "And when the Queen called and told me you'd gone to see Nick, I lost my fucking mind."

"Nicky called and asked me to meet him. I had to talk to him. I needed closure. And for the record, I didn't sleep with him or anything even close."

"I know. That's the only reason he's still . . . in existence. I'd be able to smell him on you if you had."

"Well, you don't have to worry. My virginity is safe and sound, right where you left it."

"You know I never cared that you were a virgin, right? I'm glad I get to be your first, but it never mattered to me. When I asked for the inspection, I never thought for one minute that you'd actually go through with it. I only asked for it because you were so cold and indifferent to me. I wanted to get a reaction out of you. Shake you up a little. But you were so defiant and beautiful that night, I was the one that ended up shaken. The last month, all of this." He moves his hand back and forth between us. "I've never felt like this before."

"What *is* this between us?" I repeat his hand gesture, not quite sure what I'm hoping he'll say.

"It has to be the mate magic. I want to see where it goes, what could be between us." He gives me a look so intense I feel singed. "Do you?"

I want him. *Desperately.* "Gods, yes." I smile up at him before becoming serious. "But in the interest of full disclosure, I should tell you that Nicky and I kissed." Then I quickly add, "Just once."

"I know. I can tell he had his mouth and hands on you. On your face, in your hair, and I'm not happy about it." Ash folds his arms over his chest.

"It was a kiss good-bye. That's all. Our relationship is completely over. But I had to end things on my own terms. And in person." The way I feel about Ash makes me realize I was never in love with Nicky. Not even close. Going up on my tiptoes, I wrap my arms around Ash's neck and try to pull his head down so I can kiss him.

He resists and turns his head to the side. "I can't kiss you right now. My dragon wants Nicky's scent off of you." Ash removes his suit jacket and tosses it over the back of a chair. "You need a shower."

"Seems a little much—"

"Now."

Without further argument, I sit on the edge of the bed, and take my boots off.

Ash takes my hand and we walk into the bathroom. Once inside, he grabs the bottom of my sweater and he whips it off, tossing it on the counter. My cami follows. He undoes the button and zipper of my jeans and then kneels down in front of me. Grabbing the waist of my jeans, he slowly pulls them down over my butt and hips and then down my legs.

I use his shoulders to steady myself as I lift first one foot and then the other so he can remove my socks and jeans. He throws them up onto the counter with my other clothes.

When I'm standing in just my black lace thong and push-up bra, Ash sits back on a knee and cocks an eyebrow at me. "You better tell me you didn't wear this for him."

"I didn't. These are my normal underthings," I explain hastily.

"They're fancy. I like them." Pressing his nose to the apex of my thighs, he inhales deeply and then kisses me over my panties. He pulls back and smiles up at me. "You smell delicious. Good enough to eat."

I want him to put his face back where it was, but he has other plans.

He rolls my panties down my legs and then stands to undo the back closure of my bra with a flick of his fingers. Sliding the bra straps off my arms, he leans down and sucks each of my small, pink nipples into his mouth. "Yes, you're most definitely delicious."

I shiver with excitement.

He throws my underthings on the pile with the rest of my clothes before meeting my eyes again. "You're the most beautiful thing I've ever seen. There are so many things I want to do with you."

"So do them," I whisper, reaching for him.

He steps back and turns on the shower. After testing the temperature, he motions to the shower with a tilt of his head. "Parts of you reek of vampire. Get in."

Once in the shower, I attempt to pull the door closed.

"Leave it open," he says, his hand on the door.

Deciding to humor him, I twist my hair into a knot on the top of my head.

"Get that hair wet."

"I just washed it. Do you have any idea how long it takes to wash and dry this much hair?"

He rolls up his shirtsleeves. "I know you're not standing there telling me how much time and effort you put in to go see your ex." He places his hand on the back of my neck and pushes me gently under the spray.

My soaking hair falls out of the loose knot and cascades down around me. I come up out of the spray sputtering and push my hair out of my face. "Enough. You've had your fun."

"Princess, I haven't even begun to have fun with you." His voice is full of wicked promises. "Make sure you wash anywhere he touched you."

If he's going to watch, I'll give him a show. I shampoo and condition my hair, arching my back. Pumping some body wash into my hand, I take my time washing my face and neck where Nicky touched me. Then I leisurely move my soapy hands down over my breasts to cup them. Gliding one hand down past my belly, I slip it between my legs and think about Ash's mouth on me. Desire flares in my belly.

"He didn't touch you there or there," Ash practically growls, his hot gaze shifting from my breasts to my pussy.

"Wouldn't want to miss a spot." I give him a sassy grin.

"You *are* an enchantress. In every way." Ash gives me a final lingering look before closing the shower door and leaving the bathroom.

Tonight is the night. I'm giddy at the thought of finally being with Ash and giving him my virginity. I'm *so* ready. Exiting the shower, I towel off and wrap myself in a hotel robe before heading back out to the room.

Ash is sitting on the edge of the bed, tying his sneakers. He's changed into a black running outfit. The defined muscles of his chest and arms strain against the fabric of his shirt. His shorts reveal his powerful thighs and calves.

I walk over to him and run my fingers through his hair, giving it a little tug. "I don't want to wait anymore. I want—"

He places his hands on my hips and gently pushes me away. Standing up, he looks down at me and says, "I know what you want, and the answer is no." Then he gently kisses my forehead.

"*What?* Are you serious?" My mouth falls open. "You've been trying to get me into bed, consummate this marriage for almost a month. And now that I'm ready, you don't want to?"

"That's right. I've been waiting for you since before I even came to your court. Now it's your turn. Don't pout, Princess. You only have a couple of days to go."

"Why are you doing this? Are *you* afraid of the Queen?" I ask, my tone churlish. He'd once suggested this was the reason Nicky and I had never had sex.

"No. She's going to be the mother-in-law from hell, I'm sure. But I'm not afraid of her. I am afraid of you, though. Afraid that one day in the future you'll say I didn't give you all the time you negotiated for. So we're going to wait and do this right. By the letter of the contract. It's called playing the long game." He lifts up the left leg of his shorts and slides his phone into the side pocket of the fitted liner underneath. "I'm going for a run. I'll be back in a couple of hours.

I'm in a mood now. A black, sexually frustrated mood. Hopping up onto the bed, I sit back against the pillows and cross my arms over my chest.

He pauses by the side of the bed. "Don't leave the suite while I'm gone. I've arranged extra security for you. There are two armed guards right outside the door. When I get back, I'll jump us back to Avalon. But after finding you with Nick, I need to release some energy. If I jump us now, we might end up on the wrong plane."

"I know another way you can release energy." I can't believe he's leaving me like this.

He heads towards the door and then stops with his hand on the doorknob. "No means no, Princess." Then he quickly leaves the suite.

Leaning over the side of the bed, I grab one of my boots and throw it at the door as it closes behind him.

"Lock the door," he says with a laugh.

CHAPTER TWENTY-EIGHT

AFTER LOCKING THE DOOR to the suite behind Ash, I put my underwear back on and climb into bed. Plumping up the pillows, I wiggle around on the unfamiliar mattress until I find a comfortable spot. Thinking about Ash, I slip into the quiet solitude of sleep.

I dream about our wedding ceremony, of walking down the aisle to him in the Queen's court. Unlike our real-life wedding, in the dream I'm thrilled about becoming his wife and I'm wearing an ethereal white wedding gown with layer upon layer of sheer tulle. When I reach Ash at the end of the aisle, I close my eyes as he lifts my veil. Opening my eyes once again, I smile up at him and my heart stops.

It's Nicky's face staring back at me.

And it looks exactly as it did the last time I saw it—a death mask of blood-red eyes aflame in chalky-white skin. He reaches out and grabs my shoulders, his talon-tipped fingers piercing my flesh. "You're mine."

Panic erupts inside me. The sense of needing to flee is overwhelming and yet oddly familiar. Suddenly, I realize Nicky is the silhouetted male I've been running from in my nightmares. Gathering the gauzy skirts of my wedding gown, I wrench out of his grasp and run back down the aisle and out of the court. My veil slips from my hair and floats to the ground behind me.

Running headlong through the cavernous hallways of the castle, I call out for someone to help me but there's no one in sight—Ash, my friends, my dogs, not even the Gorm are here.

The sound of my shoes echoes off the marble floors, and my breath comes hard and fast as I try to put as much distance between me and Nicky as possible. The well-known corridors and rooms I pass appear warped and stretched, as if I'm seeing them through a funhouse mirror. As I run, I look over my shoulder to see if Nicky is following me. Even though there's no sign of him, I don't slow down.

Ducking down a hallway I know will lead me outside to the stables, I take another look back to make sure he's not behind me. When I turn back around, he's standing at the end of the hall with his arms crossed, a smug smile exposing the tips of his scalpel-sharp fangs.

I turn and attempt to head back down the hallway but trip on my gown and fall to my knees. Scrambling to my feet, I grab up my skirts and try to make a break for it but am only able to take a few sluggish steps. It's like I'm moving in slow motion.

"Did you think you were going to walk away from me that easily?" Nicky asks, strolling toward me. The sound of his footfalls on the stone floor are like the clang of a death knell.

"Get away from me." I force my legs to move and take another halting step forward. But I'm not moving nearly fast enough, and his arms wrap around me with brutal force.

Terror fills my chest, making it difficult to think or breathe. "Let me go!" I shout.

Nicky drags me down to the floor and pushes me onto my back. Lunging on top of me, he presses my shoulders to the ground with an arm across my chest and thrusts a hand under the skirts of my gown, flipping them up.

Is he going to rape me? Is he going to take by force what I wanted to share freely with Ash? I ball up my fists and punch him wildly with every ounce of my strength.

He grabs my hands, pinning them to my sides as he wraps my gown around me, trapping me. Once I'm restrained, he moves down my body and his eyes meet mine as he spreads my legs.

I watch in horror as he sinks his fangs into the skin on the inside of my thigh, where his mark still resides. But there is no pleasure this time. There is only excruciating pain, the kind of agony that steals the scream from your lips. The kind of torment you'd sell your soul to stop.

He lifts his head and laughs as my blood shoots into the air, soaking the gossamer layers of my pristine white gown.

I thrash around, desperate to break free, but I'm imprisoned by my gown and Nicky's weight.

Ash's voice cuts through the nightmare, but he sounds as if he's a million miles away. "Nina, can you hear me? Wake up!"

"Ash! It's Nicky! Help me!" I cry out.

"He can't help you, Bella," Nicky says darkly. "I'm in your mind. I'm a part of you. And I'm going to make you regret trying to leave me."

I scream as Nicky bites me again, shooting his vampire venom into my bloodstream. The poison courses through my veins, setting me on fire, burning me alive.

"Seraphina, wake up! Now!" Ash yells.

My essence is pulled in the direction of Ash's voice before being pulled back into the dream. There's a tug-of-war happening over my mind. With each back and forth, the torture gets worse, as if I'm being drawn and quartered.

"Ash, I can't get away." Although I continue to fight and manage to get my hands free, my limbs are weakening as my blood flows freely from the bite wounds.

Nicky slithers back up my body. "You belong to me, Bella. I'm going to give you a choice. Come back to me and I'll close the wound and save you. Leave me and I'll let you bleed out, kill you in this dream."

Even if I hadn't fallen for Ash, I would never go back to Nicky. He's shown me his true colors. "It's over between us."

"Then you'll suffer the consequences. Because if I can't have you, nobody can." He sits back and watches me, not an ounce of compassion in his crimson gaze.

My blood forms a warm pool under me, continuing to pump out of my body. My heart skips several beats, and my eyes flutter closed as darkness consumes me.

"She's not breathing!" The urgency in Ash's voice catches my attention, but he's so far away.

A flash of pain turns me inside out and a final thought fills my mind—so much of my life is undone, including what Ash and I could have been.

And then nothingness.

Hands poke, prod and shake me.

"Wake up, Seraphina! Ash shouts again. "She's still not breathing, Sofie."

I struggle up to the surface of my unconsciousness, but something is preventing me from breaking through. It's as if I'm submerged underwater and a frozen layer of thick ice is keeping me imprisoned there, unable to take a breath. *Did Nicky kill me? Am I dead? Is this the great beyond?*

"I'm working on it," Sofie says in her calm physician's voice.

"Work faster!" Ash roars.

I pound on the barrier that separates us with my fists. *I'm here! Help me!*

The barrier thins and becomes sticky and viscous, like a layer of glue. I scratch and gouge at it, creating a hole large enough to slip through. The slimy edges of the opening cling to my skin as I push through to the other side.

Gasping for air, my eyes fly open and the overhead light blinds me. *I'm alive.*

"She's awake," Ash says, his face only inches from mine.

"Ash, stand aside so I can attend to her properly," Sofie says, trying to get Ash to step back.

"Where am I?" I ask, blinking against the harsh light.

"You're back on Avalon, in Sofie's office." Ash caresses my cheek with the back of his hand.

"You were unconscious and unresponsive," Sofie says. "How do you feel? Are you in any pain?"

Taking stock, I'm happy to find the agony in the dream no longer wracks my body. "I'm okay."

I attempt to sit up and Ash snatches me against him in a tight hug. "What happened to you?"

Returning the embrace, I savor the warmth and strength of his body before pulling back. Wearing nothing but my bra and panties, I look for any physical signs of the trauma Nicky had inflicted on me in the dream. There are none. "It was a nightmare."

Ash glides his hands lightly up and down my back. "When I came back to the hotel from my run, the guards had just broken down the door to the suite. You were flailing around the bed and screaming for your life. When I couldn't wake you, I jumped you straight to Sofie."

"I was stuck in the nightmare and couldn't wake up. It was so real." I shudder at the memory. "How did you finally snap me out of it?"

Sofie tilts her head to the door. "Ash, would you mind stepping outside so I can have a word alone with my patient?"

He crosses his arms over his chest and locks eyes with Sofie. "I'm not going anywhere. How *did* you wake her up? Nothing I did was working."

Sofie makes meaningful eye contact with me, but says nothing.

"It's okay, Sofie. He needs to know the truth." I take a steadying breath before meeting Ash's eyes. "Nicky was in the nightmare. He was torturing me, trying to kill me."

"And I did what I should have done a long time ago." Sofie exhales softly. "I removed Nicky's mark."

Ash's eyebrows draw together over golden eyes. "What the fuck is Sofie talking about, Princess? I thought that mark was removed weeks ago."

"I asked Sofie to hide the bite but keep the magic. At the time, I was looking for a way out of our arranged marriage. I thought Nicky and I belonged together. I was planning to have Sofie remove the mark as soon as we got back from Providence, but I didn't get the chance."

"If I had known you were still wearing his mark, I would never have left you alone in the suite." Ash rubs the creases in his forehead, before running a hand through his hair.

"It was a mistake to keep the mark. I know that now. I haven't felt like myself since Nicky bit me and I've been having nightmares since I came back to Avalon. I didn't tell you about the nightmares because I thought it was my subconscious warning me away from you and our marriage. Looking back, I realize Nicky bit me without my consent and then used his mark to influence me and as a gateway to my dreams." I glance between Ash and Sofie. "You two were right about him."

Ash turns to Sofie. "Is his mark fully off of her now? Is his magic completely gone?"

"Vampire magic is oily and difficult to remove, but yes, it's gone. His hold over her is broken." Sofie frowns. "This attack is my fault. I should have removed the mark as soon as I saw it."

I shake my head. "It's not your fault, Sofie. It's mine. I chose to keep it."

"I should have killed him when I had the chance." Ash rolls his shoulders back and takes a step toward the door. "I'm going back to Providence to finish the job."

I place a hand on his chest, stopping him. "You can't kill my vampire ex-boyfriend for biting me, Ash. It'll be his word against mine about consent. And he'll deny the mind control and attacking me in my dreams." I raise my arms out in front of me. "There isn't a mark on me."

Ash growls low in his throat.

"And we can't forget, he's from a royal family, too. The Council of Seven will never sanction killing him with no proof of wrongdoing. They'll consider it excessive force. They may even consider it an act of war. Sofie got rid of his magic, and he's out of my life. Can we please move on with ours?" I just want to put this whole ugly mess with Nicky behind me.

Ash pulls out his phone.

"What are you doing?" I ask.

"I'm asking the Queen to deploy the Gorm Earthside to pick him up and deliver him to the council. He needs to be held accountable for his actions even if I can't kill him. If he kept you in that nightmare any longer, he could have crushed your mind. At best, he abused his power over you. At worst, he targeted and attacked you for reasons we don't understand."

CHAPTER
TWENTY-NINE

A LTHOUGH THERE ARE NO outward signs of Nicky's attack, the fight over my mind left me with the same symptoms as a mild concussion—headache, nausea and sensitivity to light. I sleep most of the next two days to recover. Every time I wake, Ash or one of the girls is sitting in a chair beside my bed, ready with offers of food and drink.

On one of my visits to consciousness, Ash lets me know the Gorm were unable to find Nicky. Ash suspects he returned to his father's preternatural island stronghold where he's untouchable.

Ash suggests we amend the paperwork and push out the consummation date until I'm feeling better. I fervently reject his idea. As a matter of fact, I try to lure him into bed with me a few times, to no avail.

The truth is, I'm tired of waiting. Thanks to Nicky's mark and a healthy dose of my own stubbornness, I'd nearly pushed

Ash out of my life. I secretly worry he'll realize I'm a lot to take on and change his mind at the last minute.

When the big day arrives, I feel a lot better and more like myself than I have in months. I take my time getting ready, soaking in the bath, shaving my legs and scrubbing my skin until it's pink and glowing.

The Queen's personal makeup artist and hairstylist come to help me get ready. The stylist blow-dries my hair until it shines and then curls it into loose waves. The makeup artist highlights my eyes and gives my skin an extra fresh and dewy appearance. Once they leave, I put on a white bodysuit made of soft, clingy fabric. It has a deep *V* in the front, wide shoulder straps and one thin strap across the back. The bottom of the bodysuit is cut in a high thong. *The sexy bodysuit is for Ash.*

I'm checking myself out in the mirror, turning and twisting to see what I look like from all angles when Kat and Sofie arrive together, followed by Gia a few minutes later. None of them knock before entering my bedroom. What else is new?

"Can I take a few pics? You look gorgeous." Gia is barely in the room and already has her phone pointed at me.

"Sure, but use my phone," I say, picking up my phone from a nearby covered bench and tossing it to Gia. Facing the mirror so the shots capture my front and back, I strike what I hope are some sultry poses.

"Can I send a few to Ash? As a little preview?" She has a devilish glint in her eye.

"Okay. Send him a couple of the best ones." I trust her judgment.

Gia goes to work on my phone.

"Sending nudes now, are we? As your lawyer, I have to advise against that." Kat gives me a wry smile. But I know she's happy for me, even if I'm not too sure how she feels about Ash. She'd spent the last month firmly in my corner during the "I hate Ash" cage match and had done everything in her power to get me out of the marriage. It may take her a little time to warm up to him. And him to her after she hired that less than stellar team of investigators to poke around in his past.

"It's not like he's some random guy. He's my husband. Plus, I'm covered up. Mostly." I take another turn in the mirror.

"He responded." Gia is grinning from ear to ear. "A bunch of heart-eye emojis."

I slip my dress over my head and secretly smile at his response. I can't wait for him to see me for real. My dress is a white, sleeveless V-neck, with a tie belt and a tiered skirt that falls to a few inches above my knees. *The pretty, white dress is to appease the Queen.* I did wear black to my wedding, after all. I pull my hair up, exposing the zipper at the back of my dress. "Who wants to do the honors?"

Kat comes forward. "Allow me." She zips me up and steps back. "I hope Ash realizes what a lucky bastard he is." Kat, the perennial hard-ass.

"I think I'm the lucky one, Kat."

"Fine, you're both lucky. As long as he understands that we're a package deal. Where you go, we go." The hard-ass has a soft side, too.

"Of course," I say. Truth be told, I don't think Ash has any idea what he's getting into as far as the girls are concerned. But that's a conversation for another day.

I sit on the edge of my bed to slip on my shoes. Silver, three-inch heels with an ankle wrap. *The killer shoes are for me.*

Finally, I go to my jewelry box for Ash's ring. I slide it on the fourth finger of my left hand and decide I'm never going to take it off again. *Ever.*

Kat looks at her phone. "You've been officially summoned to court. The Gorm are coming to collect you."

Ten minutes later, there's a knock at the door to my apartment.

"Are you ready? Any second thoughts? Do you want us to jump you out of here?" Sofie asks.

"I'm ready. No need for an escape plan." I smile at my friends.

We leave my bedroom and head out to the living room where Gia opens the double doors to my apartment. Four captains of the guard enter. Two turn and face the doors again, and I go and stand behind them. The two remaining captains fall in behind me. The girls pull up the back of the parade. As we march to court, I feel more than a little ridiculous about all the pomp and circumstance around me getting laid. I start to giggle at the notion and then quickly swallow it, covering it up with a cough.

Stewart is standing outside the court doors and gives me a proud smile. "Princess Seraphina, they're all waiting for you inside." Then he says to the guards standing at attention beside the doors, "Make way for our Princess."

I choke up a little at the word "our" and feel in many ways that this is my real wedding ceremony. I'm going in there willingly to stand up in front of everyone and commit to being Ash's wife.

The guards open the doors, and I'm relieved to see Ash standing at the front of court, right in front of the Queen. My eyes start to well up as I think about how I almost lost him.

Ash exudes quiet confidence, looking gorgeous in a black suit, crisp white shirt and black tie with silver flecks. He smiles when he sees me, his eyes lighting up.

I give him an unguarded smile back, hoping he can see my happiness.

The Queen is on her dais in full ceremonial regalia and her consort is at her side wearing a bored expression. The court contains about five hundred of her friends and acquaintances.

The captains of the guard leave me with Ash. Standing right next to him, I feel suddenly shy. He'd almost been the one that got away. So much has changed since the last time we were here. This is the real beginning of our marriage.

The Queen looks at me with a self-satisfied air. "It appears your time has run out, Seraphina. It is time for you to do your duty for Avalon."

I fight back the giggles that have chosen this moment to reappear. "It appears so." She thinks she's bested me; bent me to her will. Little does she know, I would have willingly jumped Ash's bones days ago. "But make no mistake, my Queen." I say solemnly. "I'm here because I want to be here. Ash is *my* choice. This marriage is *my* choice."

Ash places his hand on my lower back and we stand side by side facing the Queen.

POWER HUNGRY

The Queen sits a little straighter and addresses the crowd. "Today the marriage of Princess Seraphina to Prince Ashton will be consummated; aligning the respective courts of Avalon and Westmoreland. They will be escorted by captains of the Gorm to a room of my choosing where they will remain until the task is complete."

Apparently, the Queen thinks I'm going to be difficult. *Where would she get an idea like that?* I bite the inside of my cheek to keep my laughter from bubbling up.

Looking at Ash, the Queen waves him forward. "Approach."

Ash walks the few feet that separate him from the Queen.

She folds her hands in her lap and fixes him with her cold, gray eyes. "Your plans for this consummation, they will include kindness and consideration." It wasn't a question.

"Of course," he responds immediately.

"You have a chance to make a friend or an enemy. Make the right decision. You will live a longer, happier life."

"Are you talking about yourself or your daughter?" he asks.

She gives him a closed-mouth smile before saying, "Dismissed."

I'm probably reading too much into it, but did she just show a bit of concern for me? I look up into her stoic face. *Yeah, I'm reading too much into it.*

The Gorm escort us to an apartment I've never been in before. We're in the same parade-like formation we'd been in on the walk to court, except this time, Ash is beside me. Even the girls are with us. When the guards open the doors to the apartment, Ash takes my hand, and we walk inside, leaving everyone else outside.

The guards pull the doors closed, and the giggling fit that has been threatening all day bursts free. I press my hand to my mouth, but I can't stop laughing.

"What's so funny?" Ash grins, putting his hands on my shoulders.

"This. All of this." I wave my arms in the air. "The fact that my mother just announced to hundreds of people that we're coming in here to have sex for the first time. It's ridiculous. My life is ridiculous."

"Are you nervous?" Ash asks quietly, giving my shoulders a reassuring squeeze.

I sober immediately. "No. I want this. I want you."

Ash smiles down at me, but he doesn't pull me closer or try to kiss me. Dropping his hands from my shoulders, he walks toward the French doors leading out to the balcony.

He opens both doors and steps outside. "Come out here with me for a minute, Princess."

Outside? When I step out onto the balcony, Ash closes the doors behind me. He takes my face in his hands and gazes into my eyes before giving me a long, slow kiss. Then he kisses his way up one side of my neck and nuzzles my ear. Switching to the other side, he kisses down my neck as if he's got all day, as if he's in no rush at all.

Why are we out here on the balcony?

He gently bites the muscle between my neck and shoulder, getting my attention. "You're okay with the cameras?"

I pull back and blink up at him. "What are you talking about?"

"My dragon can sense cameras in that room. I thought you knew. This is your court."

"This is the first marriage I've ever consummated, so no, I didn't know. But I shouldn't be surprised. The Queen doesn't leave anything to chance. She wants to make sure this deal is sealed."

Being a member of a royal family comes with a price. Often proof of consummation is required when royal families form an alliance through an arranged marriage. Normally, the bed sheets will do. With the cameras, I'm paying a higher price than most—the cost of my month's reprieve, no doubt. *Fuck the Queen and her incessant need to have the upper hand, to control every aspect of my life.*

Ash keeps his arms around me. "What do you want to do?"

"Nothing is going to stop me from becoming your wife." I look down at the pink diamond ring on my left hand. "We have to see it through. Give them the proof they want. Then the matter is closed and can never be disputed. Sorry, this is probably more than you bargained for." I *am* a lot to take on.

Ash places his index finger under my chin and lifts my face to his. "I've wanted to make you mine for a long time, Princess. I'll do whatever it takes. The cameras don't bother me as long as they don't bother you. We'll do enough to provide the proof they want and then have our real consummation later. In private." He gives me a tender kiss, his full lips gently caressing mine.

My heart swells, and I smile at him. Then my face falls a little as I bring up a touchy subject. "Before we do this, I need to ask you something. What if my power never comes in?"

"We'll make our own kind of magic, Princess." His tone is achingly tender.

Our own kind of magic! He doesn't care about my lack of power. He wants me for me. His words lift this incredible weight off my shoulders, and the relief is so great, I sag against him for a moment before kissing him. Hard. "You know me, Ash, I'm not opposed to putting on a little show. Let's go make a sex tape."

"Let's go," he says with a chuckle. Taking my hand, he leads me back inside to the bed, piled high with pillows and fresh white linens.

I go up on my tiptoes and wrap my arms around his neck, pressing my lips to his, our open mouths devouring each other. Putting my hands in his hair, I rub my breasts against his chest. His arms envelop me, and he presses me closer.

Pulling back, I unbutton his jacket, slide my hands inside and push it off his powerful shoulders, letting it fall to the floor. Then I untuck his shirt and place my hands on the warm, bare skin of his stomach and slowly slide them around to his back. His hard muscles flex under my touch and I move against him, hot and restless.

Staying very close to me, he whispers, "Get in the bed. Under the covers. Leave your dress on. I don't want whoever watches this to see any part of you."

I sit on the bed and remove my shoes. Then I stand, lift the covers and slide fully dressed between the pristine white sheets. Ash walks around to the other side. He toes off his shoes and strips down to his boxers. Then he says, "Fuck it" and takes them off, too.

He gets into the bed and we meet in the middle, only our heads and shoulders sticking out from under the covers. As our lips meet, he slips his hand into the V-neck of my dress, beneath my bodysuit, to palm my breast. Plucking my nipple between his index and middle fingers, he sets off a multicolored fireworks display in my body. When my nipple is taunt, he takes the same care with the other one until it, too, is standing at attention.

I'm barely able to concentrate when he begins to murmur words of praise and approval in a low voice. I can only moan in response.

He kisses my neck as his hand drifts down to where I want it most. Pushing my dress up out of the way, he cups between my legs, rocking the heel of his hand back and forth on my clit, igniting the fireworks of my desire into roaring flames. Then he stops to undo the snaps of my bodysuit and pushes it out of his way.

He eases a single finger through my slick folds until he reaches the gathering wetness at my entrance. He dips his finger into my moisture and spreads it up to my clit. Then he slowly presses his finger inside me.

My pussy tightens greedily around his finger. Keeping his finger inside me is the only thing on my one-track mind until his thumb starts massaging tiny circles around my clit. *This is what I want.* My hips start moving back and forth on their own. He continues to massage my sweet spot as he fingers me. My orgasm crashes over me unexpectedly, sinking me and I buck mindlessly against his hand.

Moving over me, Ash positions his hips between my spread legs. "Tell me you want this. That you want me."

"I did already," I answer sotto voce.

"So, tell me again."

"I want you, Ash. I want this. I want to be yours. And you to be mine," I say, looking at him with trust-filled eyes.

He notches himself at my opening and with a flex of his hips, he enters me. His eyes never leave mine as if he's making sure I'm okay.

I nod up at him, unable to speak, clutching his shoulders. Having him inside me is overwhelming. I feel very full, stretched to capacity. He pulls back and pushes in a little deeper, each time holding still for a few seconds. His cock delivers delicious friction and coaxes out the last tremors of my orgasm. Only the golden hue of his eyes betrays how much effort his patience is demanding of him.

I tilt my hips up to meet his, wanting him to move faster to relieve the slight stinging that signals I'm no longer a virgin.

"You feel amazing. Better than I could have ever imagined." He bites his bottom lip and closes his eyes as he goes up on his hands and pumps into me slowly with measured strokes.

I wrap my legs tighter around his hips to let him know I'm fully with him. His leisurely rhythm makes me feel as if I'm the most important thing in all of the planes to him.

Then he gives one final push and stills over top of me, his body rigid with pleasure. When his breathing returns somewhat to normal, he carefully pulls out of me but stays over me, balancing his weight on his elbows and cocooning me in the warmth of his body. "Are you okay?"

"Better than okay. Way better. I'm really your wife now. You're really my husband." Wrapping my arms around his neck, I pull him down for a kiss.

"That's right, Princess." He returns my kiss with a lingering one of his own. "We're mated. Together until forever."

Rolling to the side, he grabs an end of a sheet and carefully wipes between my legs. Then he snaps my bodysuit back into place and pulls my dress down before showing me the sheet. My blood mixed with his cum.

"They have the proof they want. Let's get out of here." Ash throws back the covers and quickly dresses while I sit on the edge of the bed and put my shoes back on.

As we walk out of the apartment hand-in-hand, I realize I'm not the least bit upset about how my wedding night has turned out. Was it every girl's dream for her first time? No. I lost my virginity on camera, but I gained something too. An ally. A husband. *Ash.*

CHAPTER THIRTY

AFTER ASH CARRIES ME across the threshold of his apartment, we undress and I wind my hair into a loose topknot. Then we shower together—the warm water soothing the twinges from my first time playing sexcapades.

Once we're clean, Ash wraps me up in a towel and ushers me into his bedroom. From his dresser, he retrieves a pair of black microfiber boxer shorts and a white cotton T-shirt with a rugby logo on it. After he pulls on his boxers, he positions the T-shirt over my head. I drop my towel and raise my arms so he can slide it down over me. It falls to my midthigh and has the softness of something that's been washed a thousand times. It must be one of his favorites.

Ash's breath catches as I shake my hair out. "As sexy as you look right now and as much as I want you again, I think you've had enough for one day."

My eyes travel over my new husband. Starting with his gorgeous face and then moving down over his powerful chest and shredded abs to the ropey muscles of his thighs.

I don't think I'll ever get tired of looking at him. But it's not just his outside that fascinates me, it's his inside, too. He's complicated, intelligent and honorable, while also being driven and ambitious. And remembering all of our quarrels, he never lets me get away with anything. Which I like for some reason. He's probably never going to tell me what I want to hear. But he'll tell me what I need to hear. Whether I want to hear it or not. *Gods help me.* I close the distance between us and give him an open-mouthed kiss, tangling my tongue with his. "Actually, I'm ready for round two."

He cups my breasts, rubbing his thumbs lightly over my nipples through the soft cotton. "We have lots of time for round two."

"I want my real consummation. I don't want to wait." If patience is a virtue, I'm not at all virtuous. Especially when it comes to Ash.

Dropping his hands from my breasts, he looks down at me as if undecided.

I run my hand across his chest and then allow it to drift down over his stomach. When he doesn't stop me, I let my hand wander farther south. *What the heck? Might as well go for gold.* Placing my hand over his dick, I begin stroking him over his black boxer shorts. I watch as his cock lengthens and hardens until the tip is pushing out under the elastic waistband of his boxers. Seeing him get hard by my hand sends flickers of excitement licking through me, lighting up nerve endings all over my body.

Without warning, he snatches me up and crosses the room to lay me on his kingsized bed. "Your playtime is over. It's my turn to play."

"I was just getting you warmed up." But in truth, I'm the one who's warm.

"You succeeded." He gets on the bed beside me and drops tiny kisses across the length of my collarbone, keeping my nerve endings alight. "Earlier was all about proof. This time it's going to be all about pleasure."

I wrap my arms around his neck. "I don't know about your experience earlier, but mine was very pleasurable." I weave my fingers into his hair and give it a tug on the word *pleasurable*.

Ash kisses down one shoulder to the sensitive skin on the inside of my elbow, making me squirm with delight. "There's a lot more pleasure to be had. I wasn't even all the way inside you."

I'm sorry, come again? "What are you talking about?"

Ash nips the inside of my other elbow, sending a shock of desire through me, and then trails kisses up my arm. "I held back a little. I didn't want you to scream or cry and have the whole Gorm Guard bust the damn door down."

"Well, how far in were you?" I remember feeling stretched to capacity. I'm not sure I can take much more. Then I remember the orgasm he gave me and quickly decide I can take one for the team.

"Halfway. Maybe three quarters."

Halfway! Even though this news panics me a little, I don't like the thought of him holding any part of himself back from me. He's mine, and I want all of him. "Don't hold back this time."

Ash lowers his face to mine. The kiss starts light but quickly becomes more demanding as he uses his mouth to open mine. Our tongues meet, sending shivers down my spine. When we come up for air, he sucks my lower lip into his mouth. Every pull on my lip reverberates through me with an answering throb of my clit.

My hands roam up and down his rippling back, urging him on. "I'm ready," I moan.

"Not yet," he replies, kissing down my neck while pushing his T-shirt up over my breasts. I raise my arms over my head, and he yanks the T-shirt off and throws it over his shoulder, leaving me naked.

Arching my back, I push my boobs out for his attention. He doesn't disappoint.

Taking one of my breasts in his large hand, he gives it a gentle squeeze. Then he sucks each of my nipples into his hot mouth. He teases them with his teeth, giving me just the slightest edge of pain. The edge of pain thrills me. Feeling the moisture gather between my legs, I writhe impatiently. "I'm ready," I say again, this time with more force.

"It's all about anticipation. The journey, not the destination," he murmurs into my skin as he continues to toy with my nipples. "We're going to take our time. There's no need to rush. I want you nice and wet."

"I *am* wet," I groan. "And I'm really more of a destination person."

On all fours above me, Ash kisses his way slowly down my stomach, taking the long route to kiss along my sides as well.

He's torturing me.

After placing a kiss on each of my hip bones, he says, "Let's see how wet you are then." Sitting back on his heels, his hands move behind my knees, and he pushes my legs up and back over my torso. And then he just looks at me. For what feels like forever.

"Ash, what're you doing?"

"Breathing you in. Enjoying you. Looking at you. I could look at you for days."

"Could you enjoy me with a body part besides your eyes?"

"What would you suggest?"

"Your mouth." With his eyes on my throbbing pussy, I can barely think, and my voice is shaky with arousal. "And your fingers. And your dick, of course," I say, ordering off the entire menu.

"As the Princess commands it, so shall it be done." Using one long motion of his tongue, he licks me from my opening to my clit. I almost pass out from the pleasure of it, and my legs jerk against his hold. And then he does it again. And again.

I'm panting and restless, my legs straining against his hands, trying to release some of the pleasure. He lowers my legs and spreads them wide, his hands pressing on the insides of my thighs.

His tongue flicks against my clit. Once. Twice. Three times. And then he rewards me with a steady rhythm. Having his mouth on me is more decadent than a three-hour full-body massage, a ten-layer Dutch chocolate cake and a case of Dom Pérignon Rose Gold all rolled into one.

His finger traces my entrance, which I hadn't lied was wet with wanting him. He inserts the tip of his finger, and I tilt my hips, trying to take it inside me. Then he slides it all the way in. Before I can catch my breath, he inserts a second finger, stretching me in the most luscious way. He licks my clit and finger fucks me, winding me up tight. The tension and rapture are almost unbearable. Then I break, shattering into a million little pieces, my upper body quaking with the force of my climax.

As I'm coming back from the ecstasy of a visit to orgasm town, he's kissing his way back up my body and positioning his cock at my entrance.

"I want all of you," I whisper.

He pushes inside me. Pulls back and then pushes forward again, slowly working his way into me. He's so big, and my body stretches to accommodate him once again. He does feel larger than before, but I don't want him to stop. I wrap my arms and legs firmly around him. Holding him with my body and something else I'm not ready to identify.

His movements are unhurried, feeling every inch of me and allowing me to feel every inch of him. I relax and breathe, my inner muscles clinging to him as he moves within me, pleasure taking center stage.

He fully seats himself inside me and stops moving. Gazing down at me with heavy-lidded eyes, his cock twitches with impatience, and a delightful warmth builds low in my belly. My pussy clenches, and I arch into him, raking my nails down his shoulders and arms. *I want more.* He begins fucking me again, this time with more urgency. Feeling my second orgasm approach, I tilt my hips up so he taps my clit on each downward stroke. Reaching for my orgasm, I cry out his name as the bliss takes me. *He said he'd make me scream his name. He also said we'd live happily ever after.*

My body clasps around his cock, and he thrusts harder, riding me through the euphoria. When I stop pulsing around him, he pumps into me faster. Then he gives one final hard thrust, and I feel him swell even larger before coming hot and deep inside me.

He lies on top of me, balancing most of his weight on his arms, as we both catch our breath. Then he pulls out and rolls to his back, holding me to him so that my head is on his chest and I'm tucked up against him.

Lying next to his warm body and hearing his steady breathing brings me a peace and joy I've never known before. There's something about simply being near him.

When I'm able to gather the strength, I push up off his chest to gaze into his eyes. Cupping the side of my face, he traces my cheekbone with his thumb.

I give him a sated smile. "You said you'd make me yours, and you have. The marriage contract is now well and truly fulfilled. You won."

Burying his hands in my hair, Ash presses his soft lips to mine. "On the contrary, we both won, Mrs. Mountcastle. And the games have just begun."

Smiling into Ash's eyes, I see our future stretching out in front of us. Full of possibility and the unknown. But no matter what's in store, we'll face it together. Finding Northstar, getting to the bottom of the threats against me and taking our places in our respective courts.

I'm anticipating everything that's to come when my heart starts pounding like a bass drum and a sense of déjà vu wells up in my stomach. Dark spots dance across my vision and the world becomes clouded in a green and yellow haze. Every muscle in my body tightens and then jerks in uncontrollable spasms. Convulsions seize me in pain and fear. And they don't stop for a very long time.

Continued in *Charged Up*.

THANKS FOR READING!

Thank you for taking a chance on this book. I hope you loved reading *Power Hungry* as much as I loved writing it. Let me know what you think by leaving a review. I read and ***really*** appreciate every single review!

Please leave a review on Amazon, Goodreads or both!

Thank you! :)

HEAR FROM ASH

Want to know what goes on inside the mind of a dragon shifter before he claims his fated mate? Find out in *Ashton's Story – A Dragon's Tale.*

This FREE download is a prequel to *Power Hungry*, Book 1 of The Queen's Court series and is available exclusively to my newsletter subscribers. Join today to get Ash's point of view.

Spoiler alert: When your dragon forces you to claim a pain-in-the-ass princess as your fated mate...you fight it every step of the way.

Get it here: https://BookHip.com/ZCKGCPH

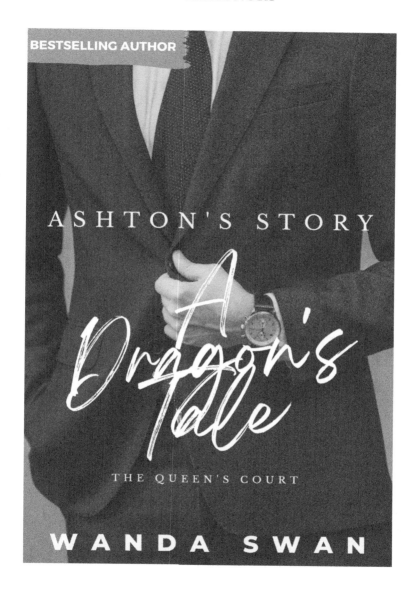

BESTSELLING AUTHOR

ASHTON'S STORY

A Dragon's Tale

THE QUEEN'S COURT

WANDA SWAN

CHARGED UP

QUEEN'S COURT, BOOK 2

I F YOU ENJOYED *POWER Hungry*, follow Ash and Nina's love story in Book Two of The Queen's Court series, *Charged Up*.

CHARGED

THE QUEEN'S COURT

UP

BOOK TWO

WANDA SWAN

ACKNOWLEDGMENTS

No one does it alone. There are so many people who helped to make this book a reality.

Thank you to my editor, Maggie Morris, for your thoughtful editing and insightful feedback.

Thank you to my cover artist, Stephanie Saw, for perfectly capturing Nina's vibe in a kickass cover.

Thank you to my proofreaders, Aislin Lynx and Megan Breininger, for all your cheerleading and confidence building.

A huge thank you to all of whose who read this book early. Much love even though I can't name you all here.

Extra special thanks to my husband and children who encourage me to follow my dreams.

ALSO BY WANDA SWAN

The Queen's Court (in reading order)

Power Hungry

Charged Up

Live Wire

High Voltage

ABOUT THE AUTHOR

Wanda Swan is an Amazon #1 bestselling author of romantic fantasy where love and passion meet murder and mayhem. She pits imperfect heroines against the odds where they must combat internal demons and external chaos to find themselves, their perfect match, and their happily ever after.

When she isn't wreaking havoc for her characters, Wanda is hiking to keep her butt firm, watching cooking shows even though she doesn't cook or daydreaming about fantastical new worlds.

She lives in small-town Ontario, Canada, with her husband, children and a Boston Terrier who thinks she's the queen of the castle.

FIND WANDA

You can find Wanda in all the usual places:

www.wandaswanauthor.com

a
amzn.com/Wanda-Swan/e/B0BFNY6ZVM

g
https://bit.ly/Goodreads-WandaSwan

⊙
instagram.com/wandaswanauthor

♪
tiktok.com/@wandaswanauthor